D1015719

Also by Robert Cohen

THE HERE AND NOW

THE ORGAN BUILDER

INSPIRED SLEEP

The Varieties of Romantic Experience

Stories

Robert Cohen

SCRIBNER
New York London Toronto Sydney Singapore

SCRIBNER
1230 Avenue of the Americas
New York, NY 10020

For information about special discounts for bulk purchases,
please contact Simon & Schuster Special Sales:
1-800-456-6798 or business@simonandschuster.com

DESIGNED BY ERICH HOBBING

Text set in Garamond No. 3

Manufactured in the United States of America

10 9 8 7 6 5 4 3 2 1

Library of Congress Cataloging-in-Publication Data is available.

ISBN 0-7432-2962-2
Some of the stories contained herein previously appeared in slightly different form in other media: "The Next Big Thing" in *New England Review,* "The Varieties of Romantic Experience" in *Harper's,* "Points of Interest" in *The Atlantic Monthly (Unbound),* "The Bachelor Party" in *GQ,* "Adult Education" in *Antaeus,* "A Flight of Sparks" in *Paris Review,* "Oscillations" in *Pequod,* "The Boys at Night" in *Glimmer Train,* and "Between Hammers" in *Story.*

For Ted Solotaroff

Contents

The Varieties of Romantic Experience

The Next Big Thing

If it had been up to Howard, he'd have been there the first day it opened. That was how he saw it: arriving at dawn, glass doors flying open with a sigh, he and Bella strolling arm in arm across the virgin carpet, entering like lords. It would not exactly be a novelty—he'd been down to Atlantic City six or seven times over the years—but possibly it would feel like one. The senses were gullible that way. They received and received and received, and still at the end of the day there was this indiscriminate hunger for more.

But it hadn't been up to him, of course. There was a long list of things that weren't up to Howard Udovin at this point. He was sixty-six years old and his business had failed. His stocks were precarious, his best friends were dead, his wife refused to take him seriously, and now there were two balloons in his chest just to keep his heart from collapsing. That was how things were. The balloons he was aware of all the time, two thin, colorless membranes upon which the unruly weight of his life depended. Children's toys. And yet to accommodate their presence required some very adult adjustments.

For instance, he'd had to liquidate the inventory. That was an adjustment. He'd had to give up smoking. More adjustment. Tennis. Coffee, scotch, red meat, peanuts, ice cream, shellfish—okay, a lot of adjustment. Even sex, which thanks to the blood thinners he'd had to give up, at least for a while, even that.

Bad luck, yes. A difficult situation to be sure. But where realities were concerned one learned to compromise. What *was* reality anyway? A leash around your neck that tightened as you got older. As for the sex, he only missed it sometimes. In bed now he just closed his eyes and lay there like a baby. Nothing was asked of him, nothing expected. That was the upside of his condition: how little was expected of him, even by himself.

And now, after that incident on the Triborough last March, he'd been relieved of his driver's license too, so if he wanted to go anywhere he had to persuade Bella to take him. This meant waiting until she was in the right mood, which it so happened was practically never. For a woman as moody as Bella, you'd think that every so often the law of averages would prevail and one of her moods would swing into harmony with one of yours. But no. Bella's moods remained obdurate; they swung on their own private hinge.

"Don't pester me," she'd said, when he approached her with his proposition. She was out in the backyard, laying down bricks end-to-end, creating an enclosure for the herb garden. There was no reason to enclose the herb garden that Howard was aware of, but it was in Bella's nature to build walls, to make fine delineations. "I'm not interested."

"Arthur Pearle went up there last week. He says the place is first rate. The next big thing, he says."

"Then go with him."

"I don't want to go with Arthur. He makes those crummy puns all the time, and he'll bore me to death about the grandkids. I want to go with you, Bella."

"Long drives make me sleepy."

"So nap on the ferry," he said.

"I nap in the daytime, I can't sleep at night."

"So you won't nap," Howard said. "You'll read. You'll do a crossword. You'll look out at the Sound and tell me your dreams."

"Ha!" she said. "My dreams!"

"Fine. I was just talking. Do what you want."

"You want my dreams?" Bella put down her brick and looked at him.

"I was just talking, Bella." Suddenly the last thing he wanted was to go anywhere with this woman. How had they even traveled this far?

"In my dreams my mother comes out of the sky, sits on the edge of the bed, and sings to me in Russian. She sings, wake up you stupid girl, wake up. But I don't."

"Bella," he said, "I was just talking."

"Sometimes it's not my mother. Sometimes it's Aunt Ida who comes, also singing, in a black fur coat. Ida the widow: she was seventeen, practically a pauper. Where did she get such a coat?"

"Maybe she hit big at the casino, Bella. Why not try it yourself?"

Bella gave an aristocratic sniff by which to indicate deep thought. She took off one work glove and considered the back of her hand for a moment, where the skin was bunched and dry from exposure, like old coral. "I don't like to leave the garden right now," she said finally. "The weather's changeable. You turn your back and next thing it's gone."

"One day, Bella."

"Things happen in less time than that."

"Things? What things? What are you talking about? Do you even know, or are you just saying whatever comes into your head to make me mad?"

"Pish tosh," Bella said. "You were always an angry person, Mickey says. Now you're more so. That's it in a nutshell."

"You're the nutshell, Bella."

Mickey the big shot. Twenty years ago he took a survey course at Brooklyn College, and ever since he's Doctor Freud. But you had to tread carefully around the subject of Mickey. He was Bella's one and only, and if he hadn't moved to California she'd still be cutting up his chicken for him every night. Also, as Bella would be quick to remind him, Howard had no children himself. The reasons for this were not entirely clear. His first wife, Fay, had wanted a family, but he was just starting out then, long hours, weekends, eating lunch at his desk so as not to miss any calls, all the time conscious over his shoulder of the cold clear eye of the bank. He'd said, wait. Give me a chance to get established; let me make a name. In truth his feelings on the subject had been vague, half-formed; it was possible, if challenged, they'd have taken a different shape. But Fay did not challenge. Poor amiable Fay, who could barely heat up a pot of coffee without encouragement, never challenged.

They waited all right. They waited until she was dead in the ground.

Anyway what difference did it make? At their age, even children weren't children anymore. They were grown-up and gone, with complications of their own. Take Mickey. Thirty-eight years old and already bald on top, already seeing doctors for mysterious ailments, already divorced. No, children didn't solve anything. Children were just a passing phase, a diversion. They were children for a while and then they turned into something else. Meanwhile you were still just you.

"Look around, old woman," he said. "We have money and time and a big car from Detroit. We're free."

Bella waved her wrist. "You don't know the meaning."

"Arthur Pearle knows. He's been to Cancún, Hawaii, Santa Fe. He says this place out in the woods tops them all. State of the art facility. There's even a museum on the premises."

"Museum?" Bella, who in her capacious and neatly ordered wallet carried membership cards for the Whitney, the Met, the Modern, the Guggenheim, the Jewish, and the International Center for Photography, perked up at this. "What kind?"

"Historical," Howard said authoritatively, though in truth he could not recall what kind of museum Arthur had said it was. "You know, Indian stuff. Native peoples, Bella. A rich and valuable heritage. It's time we stop thinking like immigrants and learn the history of the land."

"Learn your own," she said. "That would be plenty of history right there."

It wasn't going to happen, he realized that, but he could not keep himself from shouting, "I'm not talking about me, damn you. I'm talking about this country. I'm talking about opportunity, free enterprise. I'm talking about open space, Bella. About *loopholes.*" She blinked at him coolly as if she had never heard this word before, as if he were making it up. It was a common and terrifically unfair theme of their marriage that he was not as bright as she was, and thus less entitled for some reason to speak his mind. "Don't you see?" he persisted. "Every empty space is an opportunity. The Indians, they've figured this out. You get beat up and shoved aside for hundreds of years, you learn how to interpret the laws. Work the margins. Like us."

That blink again.

"They say the Indians might be the missing tribe. You know, the one that got lost in the Bible. Arthur read a theory in Book-of-the-Month."

"What book, I'd like to know. The Moron's Almanac? The Stupid Person's Guide to Life?"

"The point is," Howard kept his voice steady, "you've got to work around the limits sometimes. Take charge, change your luck. Otherwise you're just treading water."

"Dummy," she said. "My luck is right here. Why should I run off to Connecticut? I'm happy right here."

She was, too. Bella was happy right here with her bricks and short spade, her crocuses and lilies, her tarragon, chives, rhubarb, and carrots. There was no reason he could think of why she should run off to Connecticut, other than the dreary but unavoidable fact that he could not get there without her. It was a classic conflict of interest. Marriage, in his experience, was often a conflict of interest. Arthur Pearle was a widower; he could go where he wanted. Arthur had no conflict anymore, only interest. Bella and he were just the reverse. Possibly they had a bit more conflict than most. Possibly so.

Then something occurred to him. A loophole. He *could* get there without her. He'd go the same way Arthur went: on one of those cheap minibuses the casino sent around, the ones they advertised in the paper every Sunday. It would not really be his style to travel in a big group that way, but it would do, he thought.

Now that he'd been liberated from Bella, now that he did not require her for his expedition after all, now that he felt, to be honest, somewhat superior to her, more farsighted and ambitious, the way he used to feel on the road sometimes, driving a big rental car past a small industrial city over a wide gleaming elevated highway—Howard hesitated for a moment, confused. What was he doing? It was the way he'd felt after that procedure at the doctor's, the one with the balloons. This strange new pressure in his chest which was more like the absence of pressure. This strange new life to get used to. And this sense of having been ready, ready a long time, without even knowing.

• • •

The first disappointment was the minibus, which turned out to be a lot more mini than he'd supposed—just a narrow ten-seater van with a sliding door, atrocious shocks, and the casino's mauve moon logo painted on one side. When it pulled up in front of the stationery store, idling noisily and belching exhaust, Howard grimaced; he could see it was already full of old people from other stops, other towns. Not old like him, but *old.* Nine in the morning, he's wearing his good blue blazer and gray slacks, and he has to scrunch into a seat between two of the world's oldest, most annoying women.

Bella's revenge, he thought: everywhere you go you're walled in.

"You've been?" one of the women says to him. White frizzy hair piled up on her head like a helmet. Pink-rimmed glasses. Breathing hard, as if at her age even sitting down was too much exercise. She appeared to be checking out his wedding ring.

"Been what?"

"You know. Been."

"No," he says. "First time."

"We went yesterday, Charlotte and me. Yesterday was a very good day, wasn't it, Charlotte?"

"Oh, *yes*terday," said Charlotte dreamily.

"Won over fifty dollars at Keno. Fifty-*five.* Then we played the slots. Then we went and heard that black singer, what's his name, Smoker—"

"Smokey Robinson," said Charlotte.

"That's right. They let you in to watch the afternoon rehearsal if you ask, and it's free."

Howard nodded. What had he done yesterday? Argued with Bella in the backyard. Listened to the radio. Read a mystery.

The woman on his left sighed. "A very good day. That's why

we're going back. The first rule, you know, is not to mess up a good streak."

"Oh?" He waited to hear the second rule.

"And the buffet," Charlotte put in from his right. "Don't forget the buffet."

"My god." The woman on his left shook her head with a reverence that bordered on sorrow. "I swear I've never eaten so much in my life."

"Oh yes," said Charlotte.

"Charlotte had the popcorn shrimp, I had prime rib. Chili con carne. Chicken with pesto. Five kinds of pie for dessert. Plus the chocolate mousse. You tried the chocolate mousse?"

He could see there was no use in repeating how this was his first time. She had switched on her tape and it was going to loop around to its conclusion no matter what. So he leaned his head back against the seat and closed his eyes, listening to the thrumming bass notes of the tires. The road, the road. He missed it terribly. Of course he'd have preferred to be the driver, not the driven, but it was pleasant to be going somewhere for a change, just sitting back and surrendering to the machine. You could, he supposed, surrender too much. Like that time last March on the Triborough bridge. A warm night, warm enough to roll the windows down even before he got to the toll plaza, and though he'd spent most of it receiving bad news from his accountant at an overpriced Mexican restaurant on Eighth Avenue, Howard had felt, driving uptown, curiously cool and detached, as if now that the thin rope that bound his fortunes to the earthly plane of balance sheets and profit-and-loss statements had been severed for good, those fortunes were finally free to ascend, to seek out new homes in the vastness of space. Around him the city shuddered with light. There was a mild trickling noise in his head which, after the heavy meal and thunderous rock music and the six-dollar margaritas, might have been a smattering of respectful applause, the kind an arm-weary starting pitcher might hear late in the game, two runs behind, reliever strolling in from the bullpen—okay, it said, enough for now, you've tried, you've tried, you've tried. And then coming off the bridge he threw in his token, and the gate arm clicked and rose, and he stepped on the accelerator and roared the hell out of Manhattan as he used to, god, forty years back, in his golden Ford, after a night at Roseland with Fay, the car swerving beneath him as Fay herself would swerve, later, beneath the fake Utrillo in her parents' living room, and though Fay was long gone now and Howard not far behind, he succumbed all over again to the softness that seemed to lie at the center of things, the perfume that rose like breath from Fay's skin, her trembling, already-halfway-to-zaftig thighs, her clumsy and reticent mouth, and for a moment it was no longer clear to him where he was going, which way was forward and which way back, though the issue was resolved when his enormous humming front end—the Buick's, not the Ford's—plowed directly into the trunk of the Saab ahead of him.

This was followed by an interlude of loud, acrimonious, not-altogether-rational screaming, some of which Howard contributed himself. And then the tedious wait for the patrol car, the embarrassment of recounting what had happened, the ticket, the endless shuffle of insurance papers, and subsequent suspension of his license, and so on. And then having to explain it all to Bella. Very unpleasant.

The truth was he could *use* some chocolate mousse. Bella wouldn't like it but he didn't want to think about that. He did better with these dietary restrictions if he didn't think about them. Come to think of it, he did better with most things if he didn't think about them. But how to stop thinking? There was nothing he could think of to stop himself from thinking.

• • •

In Port Jefferson the passengers had to get out of the van and stand around for a few minutes while they loaded the ferry. In the shade of the terminal awning, Charlotte brought out a cigarette from deep in her purse. She must have rolled it herself—it was sloppily and anemically constructed, he thought, twisted at both ends.

"Poor thing gets nausea all the time," her friend confided in a whisper. "The chemo."

He nodded, not quite comprehending. Chemo: a shame. But what did that have to do with smoking a cigarette?

Charlotte, it turned out, had a peculiar way of smoking. Inhaling noisily from a short distance, she'd pull her head in fast, like a pigeon, to gulp back the smoke. Possibly this bizarre choreography had something to do with the tobacco itself, which smelled sickly and sweet and had a faint blue cast to its smoke, as if the product of experimental lighting.

The sky was clouding, the wind sweeping off the Sound. As they tramped onto the ferry, Charlotte began to hum a little tune.

"Who's Smokey Robertson, anyway?" he asked.

Charlotte giggled.

An hour later they were off the high violent seas and deep in the Connecticut woods, pulling into the circular driveway of the casino complex. Arthur Pearle wasn't kidding: the place really was magnificent. Teal and white, eight stories high, it rose from the entanglements of the surrounding forest like an immaculate floating city—Oz, Shangri-la—glimpsed in a dream. Limos and buses were idling in the parking lot. A crane rose and bowed in the distance. Bulldozers were at work in the woods, pushing stubbornly at the tree roots, turning things over. The whine of the motors made Howard feel coiled, itchy; his seat with its two short arms was like a straitjacket. The sight of people streaming through the revolving doors gave him a pain in his chest—a tiny flutter of the heart's wings, a kind of rising.

Trooping across the parking lot, Howard saw the box of cigarettes fall out of Charlotte's shoulderbag, bounce onto the macadam, and come to rest on its side. "Hey," he called, but nobody heard him. Old people, he thought. He stooped to pick it up: only two cigarettes left. Still, he hated to let them go to waste; he could give them to Charlotte later, he thought, for the trip home. So he slipped the box into his shirt pocket and followed the old people inside.

The Indian Casino, he saw at once, was neither so glitzy nor so vulgar as the other casinos he had seen in his life, but was more like a very prosperous and efficient suburban mall. The marble floor was as smooth as a mirror. There was a gift shop, a newsstand, a hair salon, a bowling alley, a number of restaurants. In the center of the concourse an enormous waterfall thundered over an artificial landscape of rocks and ferns. Howard looked it over thoughtfully. At the bottom was a small trickling pool in which a profuse constellation of coins, pennies mostly, shone. Howard considered throwing in a quarter, a bribe to the fates, but that seemed wasteful. The only other indoor waterfall he had seen in his life was in the lobby of the Hyatt Regency in San Francisco, on his first coast trip. He'd called Fay from the bar that night, he remembered, full of that jittery excitement of anonymity he got from the road, charging large sums to plastic accounts. He wanted to share it with her. The waterfall, the rustle of fine suits and dresses, the soft glow of the candles in their deep glazed bowls, the low murmur of lovers in their obscure assignations, the green vines dangling down the walls, just out of reach—to share all this with Fay, he thought, would make it real. He felt it in his power that night, to give all that was formless in his life shape and definition, to reach across the miles and hinge them together in the great revolving world of actual things.

But he had forgotten the time difference. At the sound of her voice, sleep-fogged and timid, his urgency faltered, and his exhilaration dissolved. The water rushed down around him, merciless, impersonal. He'd hung up the phone without identifying himself.

A thought had occurred to him: half his life was spent on the road; no matter where he was, half of himself would be missing.

Then, as if such things naturally followed, he'd ordered himself, or whoever this new self was, a double martini. A double martini for Howard Udovin! Seven bucks, and so dry it made him gasp. But the feeling was gone.

Fay, alone in that big house, a dead receiver in her hand.

Still, now that he was here in the bustle and hum of the Indian Casino, with a thick roll of twenties in his pocket, maybe the feeling could be lured back. Certainly he would not begrudge himself the money this time. Four or four hundred—what was the difference, when any minute a balloon could go pop in his chest and that would be that?

The room was long and low-slung, almost cavernously dark. Much of the acreage was given over to slot machines, hundreds of them, laid out in cheerful winding lines and clusters, like some noisy and prolifically illuminated subdivision. Perhaps because they were mindless and cheap, or because there was something in the crank and release of those heavy levers that fooled the cardiovascular system, made it think it was in fact engaged in real work, in *making* something, the slots were very popular. But Howard steered clear. He thought he saw Charlotte and her friend at the video poker, staking out stools. Good: that's who the slots were for, old ditzy ladies. He himself was here to play blackjack.

Because his instincts on fiscal matters remained conservative, Howard reflexively looked around for a five-dollar table. As it happened there were only two of them, both full. All the ten-dollar tables were occupied as well. The only vacancy to be found in the low-rent area of the casino was a twenty-dollar table squeezed into the northwest corner of the room. Well, he thought, so be it.

He pushed his way over, insinuated himself onto the stool, and handed the dealer five twenties, in exchange for which he received an alarmingly short stack of chips. He jiggled them in his palms for a moment. Not money, he thought, but almost-money. Virtual money. Arthur Pearle, the explorer, was hot on virtual reality—a promising investment, he said, the next big thing. Virtual stupidity, Bella would say. You've got enough problems with what's right in front of you; why run around chasing phantoms?

But weren't phantoms better than nothing? Wasn't it better to chase than to sit at home?

The dealer, a pleasant-looking young man with blond hair and small, expressionless eyes, cleared his throat.

"Oh. Right." With the flat of his hand, Howard pushed three chips out into the placid sea of green felt. Immediately he was hit by a wave of regret. The first play, he recalled from previous outings, was always lost; it was God's and the Gaming Commission's way of telling him to go home, stop trying to turn nothing into something. Too late now. Already he was regarding the chips through a haze of nostalgia, waving a mental farewell . . .

But in fact he was dealt two kings. Which meant his chips were returned to him, in the company of friends.

The second game he won with a ten and a nine. In the third he squeaked by with seventeen on a dealer fold. In the fourth, blackjack. Fifteen minutes, and he had won over a hundred dollars. Another half hour and he'd doubled it.

The waitress came by with her expression of perky forbearance and a tray full of drinks. She was wearing a kind of Peter Pan outfit that emphasized the musculature of her thighs and the precipitous tilt of her chest, the sight of which struck Howard like a blow. He took a scotch, neat, and, as appeared to be the protocol, replaced it with one of his chips. He was so intent on not staring at the young woman's marvelous breasts that it never occurred to him to ponder the meaning of a free drink that cost five dollars. Besides, it was a good drink. There was hardly any water. He drained it and signaled for another. He was beginning to calm down a little, beginning to feel as if the whole adventure was happening to someone else. This someone else, this Virtual Udovin, was having a pretty good time too, what with the scotch and the friendly cards and this smiling, attentive young woman whose presence was evoking what he distinctly recalled to be the first warm stirrings of a hard-on.

Here it was, just like he'd told Bella: a loophole. A little open space, exempt from the usual laws of luck and gravity, a narrow window you pried your way through and escaped into another life. And now he'd found it. Now at last the best part of himself, the winning part, the Hyatt Regency part, the roaring-down-Moshulu-Parkway-after-a-night-at-Roseland part, was able to operate freely.

Two tens. Nineteen. Dealer bust. Twenty-one. Two aces, doubled down. The other players, he noticed, had begun to exchange looks. What had been an amusing business at first had turned grave, conspiratorial. After all, they'd been present when Howard had arrived out of nowhere, uninvited; weren't those their cards, their money, he was taking?

"Canadian Club," the man next to him said wearily to the cocktail waitress. "Double."

Never once in his sporadic and unpromising career as a gambler had Howard Udovin ventured so far into the black. And yet now that he'd arrived, a dull irritation was setting in. The procession of kings and queens, aces and jacks, this extravagant royal family who kept appearing in the palm of his hand—he began to regard them with suspicion, even loathing. It was too late in the day. Too much of his life he had toiled under the shadow of fortune's moon while others went about their business bathed in light. Too much reminding himself that things could be worse: that his parents might not have escaped Europe; that the lung cancer that took Jack Dow in 1971, the brain tumor that got Herb Feldman, might just as easily have claimed him; that he had known the love of two good women, however inadequate he had been to the task; that perhaps the compromises and half-steps and mediocrity that were his life, this not-quite-this but not-quite-that-either, this interminable *middle*ness, was, when all was said and done, his destiny. And now it should change? Now he and the Indians should see how easily it could have turned out another way altogether? This was their consolation? Their restitution?

"Excuse me," he said brusquely. "I need a break."

The other players watched him scoop up his chips with expressions of bitter amusement. As if by leaving he were insulting them, flouting that first rule they lived by: never mess with a good streak. But the money, now that he had accumulated so much of it, did not quite scratch where the itch was—he still felt restless—and his bladder was painfully asserting itself. The body followed rules of its own.

Already a young man in a baseball cap, turned backward for some reason, was squeezing into his seat.

In the bathroom he emptied himself and took a long indulgent look in the mirror. All things considered, he was in passable shape. His hairline, which had given ground for years, seemed to have dug in to defend its remaining territory; his complexion was ruddy from the ferry but in no way pre-stroke; and as for the battle of his waist, that was not yet entirely lost either. There was, however, a small bulge in his shirt just above the heart that gave him a fright—was it one of the balloons, expanding on its own?—but no: the infrastructure, a patch-job, was still holding, it was just that box of cigarettes he had picked up out in the parking lot, where Charlotte had dropped it.

He had one in his mouth and lit before he could stop himself. That scotch had done its work all right. The borders were crossed, the barricades falling . . .

Funny, maybe because it had been so long, the tobacco tasted odd to him—some weird old-lady's blend, no doubt—and made him cough several times in a deep, racking way that seemed to jar something loose in his chest right where he was most tight. And yet, once the coughing fit was over, he did not feel at all bad. In fact, he felt rather light on his feet, a dandy musical-comedy version of his old self. Exiting the men's room, with the soft pop music swooning around him like cheap perfume, he felt like dancing a polka, embracing a woman, making a sale. Failing that, he wanted to eat. He was ravenous. And his mouth had gone bone dry.

Across the corridor a sumptuous buffet, a veritable cornucopia, was laid out like a vision. He got into a line with a tray. The line moved, if at all, with maddening deliberation, and because he had nothing to do and no one to talk to Howard indulged in a little philosophy. The world, he reflected, could be divided neatly in two—those who stood meekly in lines and those who crossed them. The floaters and the swimmers. Bella was a floater, he thought, and so were these people all around him. He and the Indians, on the other hand, were obviously swimmers. This was nobody's fault, just the natural order of things, ordained in the genes. Still, the important thing was to recognize what you were. To know your own nature, and act accordingly.

In time he could contain this nature of his no longer. He swam his way past the salad bar, where the congestion was the thickest, and began heaping what were arguably obscene quantities of prime rib, fried chicken, lasagna, and shrimp scampi onto his plate—all the while struggling, as he gripped the heavy ladles, to conceal his contempt for those pale dog-paddlers behind him. Look at them, he thought, flailing around at the shallow end with their cherry tomatoes and cottage cheese, their little rubbery florets of broccoli, their sensible cartons of yogurt, their quivering pastel mounds of Jell-O—picking over that lousy hospital food here, amid the plenty of the Indian Casino! In the end it required two plates filled almost beyond carrying capacity with the richest, fattiest foods imaginable, plus coffee, caffeinated, with half-and-half, *plus* chocolate mousse with its own little dollop of whipped cream, before he pulled over to the side of the pool, sated. He did not feel the least bit guilty, either. Though he went ahead and emptied a packet of NutraSweet into his coffee, somewhat rhetorically, in lieu of sugar.

"Well, well," came a voice behind him as he licked his spoon. "The man from the bus."

Howard turned. It was Charlotte's friend, the poodle. She sat alone at a table, drinking iced tea with lemon and reading a paperback.

"You're having a good day, aren't you?"

"It so happens, yes. And you?"

"Me?" She frowned. "Not so good. Yesterday was better."

"And your friend?"

"Who, Charlotte? Poor thing's lying down in the bus. Left her medication somewhere, she says. Without it she gets headaches."

"I'm sorry to hear that."

"Oh, she's very fragile. You can only do so much with Charlotte." She looked at Howard's table, the ravaged bones and scraps, the crumpled napkins and empty cups. All at once she was smiling. "You tried the mousse, didn't you?"

"Delicious," Howard averred.

"Ach, I told you. The best."

"My wife used to make some almost as good."

"Almost is almost," the woman said mildly. She cocked one eyebrow. "She didn't come with you?"

"Long drives make her sleepy. She'd rather be outdoors."

"A sensitive nature," the woman said. "You should cherish her. Show her and the children nothing but love. You'll be gone someday and at least they'll have that."

Howard nodded. It occurred to him that she must be a widow. It also occurred to him that he would in fact be gone someday. These two thoughts made him feel rather sentimental. "She's better than I deserve," he admitted.

"Why not call her and tell her?"

"What?"

"Go," the woman said. "Go call her right now. There's a phone near the cash machine."

"But," said Howard, half-rising, "what do I say?"

"Tell her the truth. Say you cherish her. Her and the children. You cherish them with all your heart."

After a big meal the blood leaves your head in a rush and shoots down to the digestive tract. Obviously it was this phenomenon, Howard thought—the whoosh of enzymes, the flops and swings of body sugars, the recessive waves of acids—that accounted for his astounding exhaustion at that moment. Even as he extricated his bulk from the table his limbs felt rubbery and stupid, and there was a strange woolly taste in his mouth, a dryness that persisted as he walked around, pockets saggy with winnings, looking for a phone. Where were they? He found totem poles, animal skins, murals, mandalas, and canoes; he found slot machines, cash machines, fax machines, a computer that connected you, via the Internet, to Gamblers Anonymous—but he could find no phone.

Too late, he remembered to ask her about the second rule, the one she hadn't told him, the one that came after the rule he'd already broken.

One of the Peter Pan girls was hurrying past with a tray of drinks. "Excuse me," he said, desperate. "A phone?"

"Pay or house?"

She was obviously speaking some kind of code he had no time to decipher. "A phone," he repeated. "To call my wife."

She made a gesture with her head that could have meant anything or nothing. He interpreted it to mean that he should descend the stairway on his left to the lower level. There he found no pay phones at all, though he did find the museum, the one Arthur had suggested might be a nice selling point for Bella. A good idea, Howard thought. It must have just been his execution that was lousy. He'd been off his form that day. That month. Still, it was worth having a look, if only so he could make a convincing report to Bella about the educational nature of his trip.

Given that he had yet to encounter an actual Indian here at the Indian Casino, perhaps it should have come as no surprise that the tribal museum was without question the loneliest and most desolate museum he'd ever set foot in. There was a small, skeletal wigwam in the center of the room, surrounded by a few halfhearted displays of arrowheads, pottery, clothing, and jewelry. Against the back wall a slide show clicked on and off, depicting in monochromatic black-and-white the long, miserable history of the tribe.

"Hi," chirped the woman behind the desk. "How are *you* today?"

She was tall and red-haired, about twenty-five, her round face complicated with freckles. A name tag on her blouse read *Sarah.* They exchanged pleasantries. He allowed Sarah to give him some pamphlets and a cheerful if unfocused little spiel. The museum, she explained, was still in progress. She herself would only be here two weeks. Then she'd be moved back upstairs to deal blackjack, which was how she made her living when she was not afflicted, as she was now, with tendonitis of the wrist.

Howard nodded thoughtfully. Sarah's syntax confused him somewhat; she had a habit of ending statements with an inquisitive upward lilt to her voice, as if much of what came out of her mouth was dubious and questionable even to her.

"It's funny," he said when she was finished, "but you don't look Indian. I thought the place would be full of them."

"Actually," she said, "they're kind of down on gambling? I think it like goes against their religion?"

"Oh. So then who runs the place?"

"Professional people. From Atlantic City? They're really good too. Another one's going up like ten miles away. The Narragansetts? It's going to be the next big one. All my friends are like let's get jobs *there.*"

He nodded vaguely. The conversation, the day, the food, his life—he was beginning to run down. He managed one lap around the room, then sought relief on the bench along the rear wall, where he sat in a slump, alone, watching the slide show flick dully past. Massacres, poverty, disease, land grabs, violated treaties, forced relocations . . . the suffering of the people, the degradation of land and spirit . . . endless. No loopholes anywhere. He wondered if the Indians really were, as Arthur Pearle claimed, the lost tribe of Israel. Wanderers through the desert, across Asia, over the Bering Strait, and then down, down, down. He wondered if history ever got tired of inflicting itself on people. He wondered if it ever took a break. He wondered if that roaring in his ears was the waterfall upstairs or the bulldozers outside or some great hidden generator beneath the floor. He wondered if the museum was kept open as the casino itself was, all night, the slides running on and on, unattended, a ghost chronicle scrolling in an empty room, a parade of transient, flickering shadows like those Bella saw wafting through her dreams, singing *wake up, wake up.* . . .

"Hey." A presence was hovering over him, distant and moonlike; he struggled up through his exhaustion to reach it. "Are you okay?"

The girl from behind the desk. There was concern in her face, but he thought he saw a number of other emotions too, whirling through the cosmos of her freckles. "Maybe you should run on home? You look kinda tired."

"I'm good," he said vaguely.

"They don't really want people sleeping on the benches."

"I'll be up in a minute."

"You want me to call someone?"

"I can make my own calls, thank you."

"Whatever," she said. "I was just trying to be nice."

It occurred to him that this was in fact the case. *Don't mess with a good streak.* "Come upstairs with me," he mumbled, trying to rouse himself. "We can have a drink and look at the waterfall."

Sarah's eyes turned hard. "Look, don't hit on me, all right? You're like older than my father. *Way* older. Also I'm having a bad day."

"That's okay," Howard said, pulling chips out of his pockets, "see? I'm having a good one."

"Not anymore you're not."

"Do you like drugs, Sarah? I think I've got some. For a minute back there I think I even had a hard-on."

"That's it," she said. "I'm calling security."

He got out of there fast. Chips spilled from his pockets as he made his way back up the stairs, past the waterfall, and into the crowded concourse. Finally: a pay phone. With trembling hands he fed coins into the slot. Then he stood listening to the tired, familiar music of the ringing of his own number. He would not tell Bella about the money, he thought. Neither would he tell her about the lunch, of course, or the scotch, or the cigarette, or the girl with the freckles. What was left? he wondered. What in the world was left to tell her?

"Hello," came Bella's voice, after the third ring. "Hello hello."

When he closed his eyes he could see her standing at the kitchen counter in her gardening gloves—looking protectively over the backyard, fretting over things left half-complete. It was as if she had forgotten him already.

He saw in that moment what was coming for them all. The next big thing.

"Bella," he said, but his voice came out a whisper.

"Hello? Hello?"

"Bella—" and he was aware of the hardware in his chest, the bloody pump and clotted channels and the thin, toylike membranes, all laboring on blindly in the darkness, "Bella," he said, "I'm here."

The Varieties of Romantic Experience: An Introduction

Good morning. It appears we have quite a turnout.

This is an elective course, as you know from the catalogue, and as such it is forced to compete with several other offerings by our department, a great many of which are, as you've no doubt heard, scandalously shopworn and dull, and so may I take a moment to say that I am personally gratified to see so many of you enrolled here in Psych 308. So many new faces. I look forward to getting to know you ea—

Yes, there are seats I believe in the last few rows, if the people, if the people there would kindly hold up a hand to indicate a vacancy beside them, yes, there, thank you . . .

Very well then. No doubt some of you have been attracted by the title listed in the catalogue, a title that is, as many of you surely know, a play on that estimable work by William James, *The Varieties of Religious Experience,* a subject very close indeed to the one at hand. I assume that is why you are here. Because, as you see, I am neither a brilliant nor a charismatic lecturer. I am merely an average one. An average-looking specimen of what to most of you must seem an average middle age, teaching at an average educational institution attended by, you'll forgive me, average students. Are there enough syllabi going around? Good. You will note right away that I subscribe to many of the informal, consensually determined rules of academic conduct and dress. I favor tweeds and denims and the occasional tie. My syntax is formal. My watch is cheap. You may well catch me in odd moments—and there will be, I assure you, no shortage of them—fiddling with this watch of mine in a nervous, abstracted way, or staring pensively out the window into the parking lot, with its perfect grid of white, dutiful lines, in a manner that suggests deep thought. You may well wonder what is the nature of these deep thoughts of mine. Am I parsing out some arcane bit of theory? Reflecting on the dualities of consciousness? Or am I simply meandering through the maze of some private sexual fantasy, as, statistics tell us, so many of us do so much of the time? Yes, there will be much to wonder about, once we get started. Much to discuss. Admittedly you may find me somewhat more forthcoming than the average tenured professor—more "upfront" as you undergraduates like to say—but that, I submit, is in the nature of my researches, and in the nature of the field itself. One must develop in our work a certain ruthlessness in regard to truths, be they truths of behavior or personality, be they quote-unquote private or public. The fact is, *There are no private truths in our world.* If you learn nothing else this semester, I trust you will learn that.

I ask, by the way, that all assignments be neatly typed. I have no teaching assistant this term. I had one last spring, a very able one at that. Perhaps some of you met her. Her name was Emily. Emily Crane.

I say *was* though of course she, Emily, Emily Crane, isn't dead. Still, I think of her as a *was,* not the *is* she surely still must be. This is one of the most common and predictable tricks of the unconscious, to suggest to us the opposite of the real, to avoid the truth when the truth will cause us pain. We will discuss such matters in the weeks ahead. We will discuss the lessons, the often hard and painful lessons, of the wounded psyche in its search for wholeness. We will seek to gain insight and understanding into our worst humiliations, not because there is implicit value in such knowledge—this is perhaps open to debate—but because as a practical matter we are conditioned more deeply by our failures than our successes, and it is vital to gain insight into what conditions us, in order that we may operate more freely.

Many of you have been led to believe just the opposite. You have been fed by the media a vulgar caricature of our profession, one that claims we are all imprinted at an early age by forces of such deterministic magnitude that we are forever thereafter obliged to repeat the same few patterns, perform endless variations on the same thin script. This is an attractive idea, of course. Like all such mystical notions, it frees us from the burden of choice and responsibility, and lays the blame instead at the feet of our parents and culture. We can surrender the struggle for well-being and console ourselves with the idea that it was never in fact available to us.

But this is nonsense. Opportunities for transformation are as plentiful as the stars, as the paintings in a museum, as you yourselves. Look around you. It's September, and I know you can all feel, as I do, the rushing of the blood that comes in with the first Canadian winds. If one breathes deeply enough one can almost feel oneself swell, become larger, less imperfect. I quite love September. I look forward to it all summer, I savor it while it's here, I mourn it when it's gone. I experience this as a personal love, but of course this is sheer narcissism—the lonely ego seeking an escape into vastness.

Those of you who have had sexual intercourse know approximately what I mean. One feels oneself changing temperature, contours; one feels an immanence; and finally one feels oneself arrive, if you will, in a larger, more generous space. One feels a good many other things too, of course, if one is fortunate.

I myself was fortunate, very fortunate, when the teaching assistantships were designated last year, and I was paired with Emily, Emily Crane. Allow me to remind you, ladies and gentlemen, that your teaching assistants should never be taken for granted. They work hard in the service of distant ideals, and are rewarded with long nights, headaches, and minimal pay. One must treat them well at all times—even, or perhaps especially, when they fail to treat you well in return. One must listen; one must attend. Certainly I tried to pay attention to Emily, to her various needs, and so forth. Her singularities. These are after all what make us interesting. Our little tics. Emily, for example, had a most irregular way of groaning to herself in moments of stress. They were very odd, involuntary, delirious little groans, and they would emerge from her at the most unexpected times. She'd groan in the car, parallel parking, or at the grocery, squeezing limes. In bed, she'd groan as she plumped the pillows, she'd groan getting under the sheets, she'd groan as she pulled off her nightshirt, she'd groan all the way through foreplay and up to the point of penetration, and then, then she'd fall magically silent, as if the presence of this new element, my penis, required of her a greater discretion than its absence. I found it disconcerting, at first. My wife Lisa, whom we will discuss later in the term—you'll find copies of her letters and diaries on reserve at the library—used to make a fair bit of noise during lovemaking, so when Emily fell quiet I had the suspicion, common among males of a sensitive nature, that I was somehow failing to please her. Apparently this was not the case, though one can never be sure. My own ego, overnourished by a doting mother—see the attached handout, "Individuation and Its Discontents: A Case Study"—is all too readily at work in such instances. But now, thinking back on Emily, Emily Crane, I find myself wondering what were, what *are,* the mechanisms that govern her responses. I wonder approximately how many small ways my perception, clouded by defenses, failed her.

Of course she failed me too. Emily was, *is,* a highly moody and capricious young woman, capable of acting out her aggressions in a variety of childish, wholly inappropriate ways. The night of the dean's birthday party last April, for example. We arrived separately of course, with our respective partners—I with Lisa, who abhorred parties, and Emily with Evan Searle, a first-year graduate student from the Deep South. Evan was tall, taller than I am, and thin, thinner than I am, a remarkably amiable and intelligent young man in every way, and so perhaps it's ungenerous of me to feel that if there were the merest bit of justice in the world he'd have long ago been the victim of a random, brutal accident. But back to the party. It was tiresome, as these things normally are, with much of the comradely backslapping that alcohol often inspires among people who don't particularly like each other. As you will no doubt observe over time, our faculty is not a close one. It is riddled with cliques and factions, with gossips and schemers and gross incompetents, and if there is anything that unites us at all, other than our dislike for teaching undergraduates, it is our dislike for the dean and his interminable parties.

This one appeared to be adhering to the typical flat trajectory. Standing between us and the liquor table was Arthur Paplow, the last Behaviorist, who subjected us to the latest in his ongoing series of full-bore ideological rants. Then Frida Nattanson—some of you may have had Frida last year for Psych 202—came over, Frida who back in her distant, now quite inconceivable youth made something of a reputation for herself by spilling a drink on Anna Freud at a party not unlike this one—anyway, Frida launched into a rather tragic litany detailing the various ongoing health issues of her wretched cat Sparky. Then Earl Stevens, our boy wonder, strode up and tried to enlist us in one of his terribly earnest games of Twister, a game cut short when our distinguished emeritus, Ludwig Stramm, fell into his customary stupor in the middle of the room and had to be circumnavigated on tiptoe, as no one had the courage to wake him. All this time, understand, I was watching Emily Crane out of the corner of my eye.

May I have the first slide please?

I have not spoken of her looks, but you will observe that she wasn't beautiful, in the classic sense, not beautiful by any means. She had a hormonal condition that kept her very thin, too thin really—note the bony shoulders—and made her skin somewhat warmer than most people's, so that she dressed in loose, floppy cotton dresses without sleeves—dresses that reveal, if you look closely, a little more of Emily than she seemed to realize. Her face was long and her mouth quite small, and this smallness of the mouth limited the range of her expressions somewhat, so that one had to know her fairly well, as I thought I did, to read her. I saw her nodding absently along with some story Evan Searle was telling to the dean's secretary. I could see that she was bored, restless, and hoping to leave early. But with whom?

I had come to the party with Lisa, who was after all my wife. We had been married for close to sixteen years. This must sound like a long time to you. And yet, when you are no longer quite so bound up in your youth, you may experience Time in a different way. You may see a diminishment in the particularities, the textures, of lived time that may well come as a relief. One could argue that this diminishment I speak of is really an intensification or heightening, closer to the Eastern notion of time as an eternal present, an unbounded horizon. Perhaps time is not the burden we think it is. Perhaps it is in fact a very light, mutable thing.

Speaking of burdens, let us return to the salient fact here, my marriage to Lisa, a commitment central to my life. I had no intention of leaving Lisa for Emily. I knew it and Emily knew it. Moreover she claimed to be perfectly satisfied with this state of affairs. She knew the score, she liked to say. I was twice her age and married, to say nothing of being her thesis adviser, and it required no special sophistication to regard what we were doing together as the predictable embodiment of an academic cliché. Of course this did nothing to diminish our excitement. Far from it. Indeed, one might argue that in our media-saturated age, eroticism is incomplete without its corresponding mirror in one popular cultural cliché or another. Has it become a cliché, then, to engage in oral sex on one's office carpet, five minutes before one's three-thirty seminar in Advanced Cognition? Of course it has. And is it a cliché to find oneself, during a recess in the Admissions Committee meeting, licking the hot, unshaven armpit of a twenty-four-year-old Phi Beta Kappa? Of course it is. Ladies and gentlemen, allow me to say that I wish such clichés on all of you. Let me say too that if they have already come your way, you will have ample opportunity to make use of them, either in class discussion or in one of the three written papers I will ask of you this term.

To continue our inquiry, then, into the events of the party: Sometime later, close to midnight, I saw Emily disengage herself from Evan Searle and wander off by herself in the direction of the kitchen. It so happened we had not been alone together in some time. Emily was busy studying for orals, and claimed to have an infection of some sort that rendered her unfit for sex. It was difficult to imagine any germ so virulent, but never mind. I did not press the point, even when the days became a week, the week ripened and then withered into a month. Oh, I called a few times, to be sure, merely to check on her health. In truth she sounded rather wan. Several times I had the distinct impression that I had woken her up, or perhaps interrupted some strenuous bit of exercise. Afterwards I would sit in my study, pour myself a finger of scotch—sometimes a whole handful—and stew in the darkness, utterly miserable, thinking of Emily, Emily Crane. The lunatic's visions of horror, wrote the great William James, are all drawn from the material of daily fact. All my daily facts had been reduced to this: I sat there alone, in a darkened room cluttered with books, a darkened mind cluttered with Emily. Emily with Evan Searle. Emily with Earl Stevens. Emily with the director of off-campus housing. Emily with delivery boys, meter maids, movie stars. Emily with everyone and everyone with Emily and nowhere a place for me.

But perhaps I have strayed from our topic.

We were still at the party, as I recall. Emily had gone into the kitchen, and I had followed. The kitchen was gleaming, immaculate, empty of people. For that matter it was empty of food. The dean, famous for his thrifty way with a budget, had hired a rather puritanical catering crew whose specialty, if you could call it that, was crustless cucumber and avocado sandwiches. Apparently Emily had not had her fill. The refrigerator was open and she had bent down to rummage through its sparse contents. She did not hear me approach. I stopped mid-step, content to watch her at work—her pale bare shoulders, her tangled coif, her air of concentrated appetite. At that moment, class, it struck me with a profound and singular force: I loved Emily Crane, loved her in a way that both included and transcended desire, loved her in a way that brought all the blockish, unruly, and disreputable passions of the self into perfect, lasting proportion. Feeling as I did, it seemed incumbent upon me to let Emily know, that we might validate together this breakthrough into a higher, headier plane of affection. And so I stepped forward.

Perhaps I should say I *lurched* forward. Apparently I'd had a bit more to drink than was strictly necessary. Apparently I'd had *quite* a bit more to drink than was strictly necessary. I'm certain a good many of you know how that feels, don't you, when you get good and ripped, and that very pleasant little brass band begins its evening concert in your head, and the baton begins to wave, and the timpani begin to roll, and one feels oneself swell into a kind of living crescendo. There's nothing quite like it. It's different than the rush one experiences on very good marijuana, say, or opiated hashish. It lacks the vague, speedy flavor of the hallucinogens. No, if it can be compared to anything I'd say it's closer, in my opinion, to fine cocaine.

Do you young people still do cocaine? It's lovely, isn't it? Emily and I liked to snort it off a moon rock she'd bought from the Museum of Natural History in New York. The dear girl was absurdly superstitious about it. We *had* to be in the bathtub, Mahler *had* to be on the stereo, the bill we used *had* to be a fresh twenty, etcetera etcetera. As you can see, she displayed a marked predilection for controlled behavior, did Emily. Alas, my own predilections run in rather the opposite direction.

As I said, I lurched forward. Emily crouched before the white infertile landscape of the dean's refrigerator, unsuspecting. All I wished to do, you see, was press my lips against the fuzzy layer of down that ran like an untended lawn across the chiseled topography of her shoulder. That was all. There must have been some form of internal miscommunication, however, some sort of synaptic firing among the brain receptors that went awry, because what proceeded to happen was something quite different. What proceeded to happen was that I stumbled over some warped, wayward tile of linoleum, and went hurtling into Emily, and the point of my chin cracked—hard—against the top of her head, which sent her flying into the refrigerator. I might mention, too, that at some point in the proceedings my pants were no longer fastened at the waist but had slipped a good deal closer to my ankles, revealing a rather horrific erection I'm at a loss to account for. Where do they come from, these erections? Does anyone know? Why do they come upon one during bus rides, for instance, but not on the train? It's a subject worthy of exploration. Some of you may well decide to undertake it, in fact, for your first paper.

Emily, for her part, began to scream. One could hardly blame her, of course: I'd caught her off guard; I'd clumsily assaulted her; I'd invaded her space, as she liked to say. I'd done everything wrong, everything. She stood there, crimson-faced, fingering the teeth marks in her skirt, her mouth—

Sorry?

Oh yes, I seemed to have bitten her skirt. Did I leave that out? An odd involuntary response, but there you have it. I still have a piece of it somewhere. A light, summery cotton material, as I remember. Sometimes I'll pick it up and pop it in my mouth again, and the effect, if I may make so grand a claim, is not unlike Proust and his madeleine, conjuring up Emily in great rushing tides of sensory detail. *Remembrance of Flings Past,* if you will. Yes, a wonderful souvenir, that bit of skirt, to say nothing of its usefulness and durability as a masturbatory aid. But I am getting ahead of myself.

Emily was screaming. That was unfortunate, of course, but not unreasonable. The disconcerting part was that even *after* she had turned around, one lip fattening and starting to bleed; even *after* she had seen that it was only me, that it had obviously all been an accident, only an accident, one that had caused me too a great deal of pain; even *after* I had begun to stammer out a lengthy and perhaps in retrospect not entirely coherent apology; even *after,* class, even *after—Emily continued to scream.* In fact she screamed louder. It was a scream without words, without inflection, as insensate and maddening as a siren. It appeared to come from some hot, awful, violent place inside Emily that I had not as yet explored . . . a place that I'll confess intrigued me. For a moment I had the completely insupportable idea that it bore some relation to her muteness during the love act, a place of inverted pleasures and projected pain, a place where all of Emily's emotional dysfunctions had sought out a refuge. Ladies and gentlemen, can you blame me for my interest in this young woman? She was fascinating, neurotic, convoluted, thoroughly extraordinary. No, I don't believe I can be blamed, not in this case, not with Emily Crane. My intentions were innocent ones, therapeutic ones. I wish to establish this point, my essential innocence, right here at the outset, because I will in all likelihood be making reference to it as the semester goes on.

There will be—did I mention?—a midterm and a final.

Of course they all came running at once, the entire faculty, including spouses, secretaries, and administrators, all came at once to the kitchen to see what had happened. For all they knew there had been a murder, a fire. How could they have known it was only a brief, botched kiss?

In time she began to calm down. Emily Crane, she calmed down. The vein at her temple softened and receded, her hands unclenched, her color assumed a normal shade. For the benefit of the onlookers she attempted a shrug of casualness, but her shoulders remained tight, unnaturally so, where I'd tried to kiss them, so that she appeared to have frozen midway through some strange, inelegant dance step. She opened her mouth to speak but nothing came out. Frida, cooing, stroked Emily's forehead. The room hushed. Emily looked at me softly, inquiringly, as she used to look at me during our Special Topics seminar only a year ago, her brow creased, her head cocked at a steep angle, her eyes wide and damp, and when she opened her mouth again I heard a whole robed choir of ardent angels rising to their feet.

"You're disgusting," she said. This in a loud and brittle voice. The sort of voice, class, one should never use on one's lover—and yet in the end one always does, it seems.

My tenured colleagues slipped away at once, grateful for the chance to escape and preoccupied, no doubt, with dramas of their own. But the junior faculty looked on greedily, their faces lit by the kind of ghoulish pleasure with which small children attend the dismemberment of insects. They'd be dining out on this for weeks. Already I could hear the first rough whispers, the first conspiratorial murmurs. Emily, if she heard them, paid no mind; she stood proud, a high priestess conducting a ritual sacrifice, slitting the throat of our love on the party's altar. "You're disgusting," she said again, perhaps for the benefit of Herr Stramm, who had missed it the first time. And then she wheeled, grabbed Evan Searle by the elbow, and commenced what I judged to be a rather theatrical exit.

Excuse me, but there are, I believe, a few minutes left.

Emily, Emily Crane, left this university soon afterward. I cannot tell you where she went because no one will tell me. It was the end of the term and I was left without a teaching assistant, left to grade one hundred seventeen undergraduate papers, which I read, quite alone, on the floor of the unfurnished apartment that Lisa insisted I sublet the week after the dean's party. No doubt in a few weeks I will be grading your papers on that same floor. Sometimes it is all I can do to rise from that floor. Sometimes it is all I can do.

"There are persons," wrote the great William James, "whose existence is little more than a series of zigzags, as now one tendency and now another gets the upper hand. Their spirit wars with their flesh, they wish for incompatibles, wayward impulses interrupt their most deliberate plans, and their lives are one long drama of repentance and of effort to repair misdemeanors and mistakes."

Who are these persons, you ask? You see one of them before you. If you take a moment and look to your left and your right, you will see two more. And by the time you are older, and not so very much older at that, you will begin to see him or her in the places you have not as yet been looking: in the reflection of a glass, say, or an intimate's stare, or a barren refrigerator. Ultimately, you see, the private will win out. The axis of reality, James tells us, runs solely through the private, egotistic places—they are strung upon it like so many beads. We are all in this together, ladies and gentlemen, in a way that would be horrible were it not so comic, but in a way that manages to be quite horrible anyway. We are all students of desire. We arrive at class eager as puppies, earnest, clumsy, groping for love. That is what brought you here this morning. You have caught the scent of possibility. You have begun to gnaw at your leashes, and they have begun to fray, and soon, soon, you will go scampering off in search of new ones.

Very well then. We are out of time. Next week, according to the syllabus, we will turn our attention to Janice, Janice Rodolfo, who left me for the captain of the golf squad in my junior year of high school. Among other issues, we will explore the theoretical implications of submissive behavior—mine—and analyze the phenomenon known as "dry humping" for its content of latent aggression. Until then, I ask only that you keep up with your reading and, of course, your journal, which I intend to review periodically. I ask that you keep your writing neat.

Are there any questions?

No?

I thought I saw a hand up . . . there, in the back row, the young lady with the red blouse, with the—

I thought I saw your hand.

Perhaps I have already answered your question. Or perhaps you're somewhat shy. There's something inhibiting, isn't there, about a forum such as this, all these narrow desks in their rigid lines. If I had my way in things, if it were up to me, this class would not be a lecture at all, but a succession of individual consultations in some small, comfortable room. A room like my office, for instance, on the third floor of this building, to the left of the stairs. Room 323. If it were up to me, young lady, you would ask your questions there. You would put down your pen and take off your shoes. There would be music, something chastened and reflective, to facilitate our inquiries. In the end we might choose not to speak at all, but merely to gaze into a flickering candle, attending to the gyrations of the light, to the dance of its shadow up the wall and to the small elusive effects of our own breath . . .

Yes?

Right, right, by all means, mustn't run over. It's only . . .

I thought, I thought there was . . .

I thought I saw her hand.

Points of Interest

GERALD

It was a homework assignment. I know it sounds ridiculous, but that's all it was.

THEA

You know, he said, like Ms. Meyott gives you at school and you're always leaving crumpled at the bottom of your backpack and forgetting to do? That kind. He was always studying. He'd get these big books from the library and we wouldn't see him for the rest of the weekend. Mom would be like, all right, let's go into the city and see a show, just us girls. I think she kind of liked having me to herself at first.

GERALD

It was an intermediate class, and I had zero experience. I felt I had to work extra hard to catch up.

THEA

Mom said we had to do our best to be supportive, he was just trying to improve himself. How come? I said. Then her eyes went funny. I wondered if she was thinking about that last report card I got from Ms. Meyott. I wondered if she was thinking it's weird how ever since he lost his job he's so into learning stuff and like I'm so not.

GERALD

How many times do I have to say this? A job is not something you up and lose one day. It has to be *taken.* It involves a lot of planning and detail work on the part of people with more power and brutality than yourself.

THEA

Anyway, it's gone.

GERALD

I admit it wasn't easy at first. There's a tendency to feel somewhat unanchored. To drift.

THEA

And ever since then it's been really weird. Like the two of us are stuck in the wrong bodies or something. I mean, *I'm* the one who's supposed to be taking piano and photography class and going to art museums on the weekends. He's supposed to be lying around in his undershirt watching game shows.

GERALD

I find that people tend to make stereotypical assumptions about the unemployed. You'd like to think your own family would be more understanding.

THEA

What's his problem, anyway? Do you know?

GERALD

You begin to search. You begin to cast around for a new direction.

ROBERTA

I had no idea. How could I? It was just a homework assignment. Perfectly pedestrian. I've been giving the same one for years.

GERALD

Roberta, in all honesty, assigned a number of things for homework that fell into the category of weird. It's her style to be provocative. Every artist has to have a little capacity for outrage, she told us. You have to cut through the bonds of sentimentality, step outside the conventional perceptions. You have to train yourself to see what's really there.

ROBERTA

I like to write something on the board that first day, when they first come in and take off their coats . . .

GERALD

Art's true subject is the human clay. She wrote it up on the blackboard and then stared at us over her deli cup of tea and lemon, as if she was daring us to ask what it meant. We hadn't even taken off our coats yet. Later, at the end of the lecture, she explained that it was from a letter that W. H. Auden, a famous homosexual poet, had written to Lord Byron. I found this a little confusing, since it was my impression that Lord Byron had been dead for centuries and here he was still receiving mail. Anyway, she was a terrific teacher, I could see that right off. A real gift. The world, she said, is full of riches. You just have to open your eyes.

THEA

Mom says not to worry. The judge is a nice man, a reasonable person. He'll be home soon and things will go back to being how they were.

GERALD

Let me take a second to point out that Roberta has been teaching this same course for six or seven years now. That her work appears in galleries all over Europe.

ROBERTA

Berlin. Amsterdam. Madrid. We're negotiating with a small dealer in Prague. Locally, there's the ICP, ICA, MOCA, the DIA, P.S. 1 . . .

GERALD

You can see it in the way she carries herself. There's a posture, a bearing, a kind of physical charisma when someone knows what they're about, when someone's on the move. I had it myself for a couple of years, I think, when I first got out of graduate school. I used to run around the city in this beautiful leather bomber jacket. I felt like a flyer, an ace. I felt like a lover. I think I was wearing that jacket the day I first met Nancy.

ROBERTA

. . . two NEAs. A CAPS, a NYSCA, a Siskind, a Ruttenberg. Shortlisted last year for the Prix de Rome. Didn't get it, but look who they picked. I mean, come on. Everyone knows how political *that* is.

GERALD

Also let me cite the fact that on the physical plane alone she is a formidable presence, Roberta. She's five ten and stocky with a buzz cut. Wears nothing but black, eats organically fed meat. There's a diamond stud in the middle of her chin, the point of which I don't even want to speculate. Who argues with such a person?

ROBERTA

That? Let's just say that it signifies an attempt to break through the usual gender dichotomy of victim and victimizer—taking control of the picture, if you like. What the French call *l'écriture féminine.* You've read Cixous? Oh, forget it . . .

GERALD

Maybe you've seen the clippings from *ARTnews* and *Artforum.* They're very effusive. Not that I'd heard of Roberta myself, of course, when I first saw her name in the catalogue. But I'm a bad example. I drew blanks on Stieglitz and Moholy-Nagy and Cartier-Bresson, too. Man Ray I thought was a kind of fish. They don't refer to such people at business school, even in the Ivy League. They just don't come up.

ROBERTA

I let all kinds into my class. Old people, junkies, housewives from Jersey. Bennington grads. My philosophy is equal access. Open admissions. Though of course I try my best to weed out the yuppies.

GERALD

She asked me why I wanted to take the course. She didn't like it that I was wearing a suit, I could tell. But I told her the truth.

ROBERTA

He mumbled something, I can't remember. Some utter bullshit about dreams.

GERALD

I said that I'm one of those people who has trouble remembering their dreams in the morning. I thought this was a sign of limitation. It seemed important to try and have some dreams when I was awake.

ROBERTA

Then as I was putting on my coat someone came up and said they had a scheduling conflict and suddenly I had this space open. He was still just standing there. Kind of a puppy dog effect, if you know what I mean. He was going to follow me home, I thought, if I didn't let him in. So I let him in.

GERALD

I went out and bought a 35mm Leicaflex SLR, a Vivitar 283 flash, and a hundred rolls of Kodak Tri-X black-and-white film.

ROBERTA

I tell them not to worry too much about the equipment. There'll be plenty of time for that later.

GERALD

The Hasids on Forty-seventh Street were rude to me at first. Then they saw the gold card. They saw the half-dozen catalogues I'd cross-referenced. They saw the three different issues of *Consumer Reports,* circled and starred. They saw that we were going to do business.

ROBERTA

The first few weeks I tell them not to worry about the technical aspects. I want them to find their material first. Their *true* material. This requires some clear-eyed investigation of their own lives, what Walker Evans called "the search for a usable past." It can be a little scary for some.

THEA

He started looking over old albums. He'd get kind of moony at dinner about all the great weird stuff he did when he was in high school. Like I guess he was some kind of hippie or something. He had a lot of hair. He used to hitchhike a lot, he said.

GERALD

I used to do a fair amount of hitchhiking. I don't remember why. The summer I was nineteen I hitched all the way to San Francisco. I don't remember why I did that, either.

THEA

Mom kept rolling her eyes, like big deal, you know? Old news.

GERALD

I remember empty roads. Gas station johns. Moldy socks. The weight of my backpack. I remember all the signs I scrawled on ripped-up cardboard that the wind blew away.

THEA

Knowing him, I doubt he was a very good hitchhiker.

GERALD

To be honest, I was not a very good hitchhiker. I didn't have the patience, the calm. I just couldn't stand there and not care where or how I was going. Even when I finally made it to San Francisco, I got lost in the middle of Golden Gate Park and wound up drinking tea in the Japanese gardens with some Australian kids who'd devoted their lives to following around the Grateful Dead, and then later we smoked some hash and fell asleep in a grove of eucalyptus, and there was this girl with a funny accent and practically nothing in the way of breasts whom I thought I was going to have sex with but didn't. The next day I turned around and started hitching home. I never even saw Chinatown. I never even saw Fisherman's Wharf. An amazing waste of time, now that I think about it.

THEA

Julie says I'd be good at it because I'm lazy and I like to hang out a lot. She says it's different for girls, though.

GERALD

Lately, though, I've been thinking about that trip. I've been wondering why at a certain point you lose the feel for that kind of thing. Why the time passes so quickly without it. Why, at a certain point, you can't even remember what possessed you to do it.

THEA

He said, let's take the afternoon off and have milkshakes. Rocky Road, he said.

GERALD

A hot day. There was some ice cream in the freezer. I don't remember what kind.

THEA

It turned out to be vanilla.

GERALD

I was out in the backyard, reading a book of theory that Roberta had put on the syllabus. Nancy was at her office. Thea and her friend Julie from down the street had some kind of noisy production going with the sprinkler. It was a hot afternoon. The grass was high and thick. The book talked about different ways of seeing. How the relation between what we see and what we know is often so unsettled. It talked about how the experience of watching the sun set never quite *fits* with the explanation that it's really just the earth turning away. That sort of thing. I realized I felt that way a lot. Watching Nancy undress for bed, for example, always makes me tense. It's as if the idea of my wife and the fact of her body are two very different things somehow, and there isn't room for both of them at the same time.

Then I heard Thea yell out that they were thirsty. I thought, what the hell, give them a treat. It was my call; I was the one doing the parenting, as we call it. I was the one doing most of what we called the parenting those days.

THEA

He'd pick me up from school. He'd do the grocery shopping. He'd go to the bank, the post office, the drugstore, the dry cleaners. He'd cook the dinner.

GERALD

Being unemployed, it's a lot more work than you think. You need a reliable car and a head for details. Plus the shame, of course, which is considerable. The shame of always being around so much.

THEA

Julie kept asking, why is he always around so much? But I was used to it by then, I guess.

GERALD

I feel sheepish admitting this, but in the old days I used to go in early to the office sometimes, earlier than I had to. There was no particular reason. I just liked the feeling of being there—alone at a clean desk, no cracker crumbs or crayons, no background noise. Just sitting in a cone of my own light.

THEA

Besides, sometimes he was really nice to have around. He'd give us treats and stuff. The milkshakes, like that was *his* idea, not ours. Mom would have given us yogurt. Nonfat.

GERALD

I went into the kitchen and got out the ice cream and milk. It had been so long since I'd had a milkshake, I couldn't remember what else was supposed to go in. The blender was a little crusty at the bottom; I tried to remember the last time we'd used it, and couldn't. It occurred to me that maybe this wasn't such a good idea after all. I might wind up poisoning everyone. But we really wanted milkshakes that day, so I went ahead and made them.

When I came back outside with the blender and three glasses on a tray, Thea and her friend were sprawled out on their bellies on the tall grass, still wet from the sprinkler, giggling about something.

THEA

Julie was telling me about this thing she found in her mother's drawer. By the bed.

GERALD

And then, I don't know, there was something about the way they looked that made me think: remember this. The light, the bees humming in the grass, the lazy inconsequential flow of the afternoon, and your daughter, your irritable knock-kneed nine-and-a-half-year-old daughter, who will never be just this way again, just this tanned and skinny and unself-conscious, this careless . . .

THEA

She said, hey, what's he doing?

GERALD

I didn't think about it after that. It was all reflex. We were seven weeks into the course by then, and maybe that day for the first time I was beginning to get it, you know? To *feel* it. The lens was starting to move inside me now. It wasn't some idea any longer but an impulse. A kind of itch.

THEA

Oh, that? He's been into that for a while now, I said.

GERALD

I forgot to say that I hadn't done that week's assignment yet.

ROBERTA

A documentary of your work environment. The assignment was broadly defined. You have to leave the parameters loose. The last thing you want to do is restrict anyone.

GERALD

Of course I *had* no work environment at the time. Which was a problem. It was getting to be a very serious problem, in fact. You might say I'd slid a bit toward the depressive end of the spectrum. Nancy wasn't being such a great sport about it, either. She began to make remarks about my weight, my hair, my libido. Remarks about shrinks. Remarks about lawyers. I don't think she meant anything serious by them, but I can't deny they had an effect.

ROBERTA

They begin to look at their own lives a bit more closely. The idea is to heighten their perception of external realities.

GERALD

You know what it's like to be unemployed? It's another country. Another country with another language and another climate, with a population made up exclusively of old people, children, and the occasional adulterer. You're not sure what the laws are. You don't know how the money works. You don't know where to eat lunch. You don't know when your visa will expire. But after a while you get used to not knowing. And that's the scary part. The way you adjust. The way after a while not knowing starts to seem almost like knowing.

THEA

I was just happy to see him excited for a change. He'd been having kind of a hard time.

GERALD

Then out on the lawn it struck me: this *is* my country. This lawn, these trees, those girls. This *is* my clay. This *is* my goddamned work environment.

THEA

I told her, don't even look at him. Just ignore him and he'll go away.

GERALD

The first roll I shot from behind. The sun had dipped a little, and the weeping willow was creating some minor havoc, shadow-wise. I began to worry if there was enough exposure.

THEA

He started walking around us in circles.

GERALD

I decided to bracket around the meter. I used three different exposures. I was concerned that details would be lost. I remembered to adjust the f-stop to ensure consistent depth of field.

THEA

Julie was getting a little nervous. Think we should put our clothes on? she said. I just laughed.

GERALD

The girls were glowing from backlight. Everywhere I pointed, the frame just filled up with them. I switched to a telephoto. I wasn't aiming at their faces, only their legs. Not even all of their legs. I shot two rolls on the backs of their knees alone. Then I kept going.

THEA

He said, hey, guys, do me a favor . . .

GERALD

I wanted to see how it would look if they turned over and the light fell directly onto their faces. First I tried stooping down. That didn't quite do it, so I went for the flash. I was thinking of those old Marlene Dietrich movies, the way they'd light her face from above, those luminous rises and hollows. I thought maybe I could do something like that. So I put the flash up as high as I could. Then I took off the telephoto and got out the macro. I went in close.

ROBERTA

Cartier-Bresson calls it "the decisive moment." When the action captured in a photograph and its abstract composition come into dynamic tension.

GERALD

Very close. I was right up under their necks. For a second, none of us moved. It was as though we all sensed that something important was happening. The girls were no longer girls. They weren't Thea and her friend Julie from the fourth grade. They were something else now, something not quite personal, but larger, stranger, altogether different. *Other,* Roberta would say.

ROBERTA

To trap the object at a given moment. The technique and the object become inseparable. The object is the technique and the technique is the object.

GERALD

. . . it wasn't even human, what they were. It was like they were just extensions of my arm, my eyes. They were these long, slender, marvelous forms, sort of like moonscapes, bumpy in some places and smooth in others, and it was all going to pass if I didn't do something very fast. I felt I needed to get them inside the frame somehow so they wouldn't disappear.

ROBERTA

The proof that something was there and no longer is. Like a stain.

GERALD

A confirmation.

THEA

Julie finally said, this is boring. I'm going home. I said, what about the milkshakes? But she was already gone.

GERALD

And that was it, really. That was the whole thing. But I had the strangest feeling later on. It was like I used to feel sometimes after sex with Nancy, a calm after the storm. It's hard to capture in words. I guess it's just the sense that for a change you've taken part in things the way you're supposed to—that just for a moment, you've been the center of it all and everything around you was just another piece of the same thing. And you too, you know? You too.

THEA

They were all warm and runny by now. I didn't even drink mine; I just left it for the bugs and went in the house. Mom came home at six, and we had burritos, and I forgot all about it. It wasn't till a week or so later, when the police guys showed up, that I even remembered.

GERALD

I was still worried about the exposure, so I told the clerk at the photo lab to push the film. Probably that's what got his attention. A very disturbed individual, that guy.

ROBERTA

I tell them at the end of the term: if you're serious about continuing, you'll need to set up a darkroom of your own. You don't want to have to be depending on someone else.

GERALD

Things got very messy after that. What with the police, and the lawyers, and the judge, and the psychologists, and the preliminary hearings, and Nancy . . . It's really difficult to overstate how messy things got after that.

THEA

They say the judge might let him come home next week. Pending, they say. Whatever that means.

GERALD

Me? Oh, fine, fine. Nancy has been very supportive, in her way. Nancy has been a real trouper. The thing is, I'm worried about Thea. What has she learned from all this? What is she going to think of me? I don't know, maybe I really did do something wrong that afternoon. Maybe I did stray across the line. But *whose* line? Do you know? Because I can't seem to find a line of my own.

THEA

Everyone keeps asking how I'm doing. It's really boring. Once a week I have to meet this lady from county services. I'm fine, I say.

Don't worry about me. Worry about *him.* Worry about *her.* Worry about *Julie.* They're the ones having trouble.

ROBERTA

What do you expect? Apologies? Listen, art is de facto subversive. By making so much of its own reality, it breaks the chain of the realities around it. That's just how it *works.*

THEA

Julie says it's on account of the cicadas last summer. They do something to the air, she says, some electrical thing that messes up people's heads. I think maybe she's right. I mean, you've got these little bugs buried in the ground for seventeen years, and then one day they all just pop out buzzing like crazy, and every time you walk you hear this crunching in the grass from all the tiny skeletons . . . You can't tell me that's *normal.*

But then when we did our science unit, Ms. Meyott said everything that happens in nature is normal. Even the very strange things, she said, like hail, and fireflies, and those huge Komodo dragon lizards you see in the zoo. Ms. Meyott has a master's degree and a birthmark on her cheek that looks like Australia. Even Julie thinks she's a smart lady. So now I don't know *what* to believe.

GERALD

You should see the letter she sent last week. Lizards, dragons—the poor kid is obviously having a rough time. Still, it was nice to get a letter from her. One thing about families is you're so close to people that you lose perspective. I mean, Thea's my own daughter, but I never knew until now what a letter from her would look like.

THEA

Mom says we have to help each other through the rough patches, even when we don't understand. *Especially* when we don't understand.

GERALD

The thing is, I still haven't seen the photographs. Have you? Do you think they'll let you take a look? Because the way things are going, I may *never* see them. But that's okay, in a way. That's okay. Somewhere out there are a hundred and forty-six pictures I shot that afternoon, and one or two of them might be really good. Maybe even exceptionally good. And that's enough for me, for now. Just to know that it's possible. Just to know I was able to capture a few moments in time like that, instead of it being the other way around. That I put myself into the picture a little. That's enough.

THEA

I didn't understand most of his letter, to be honest. He said he was beginning to think a different way than before. He said it could turn out to be a blessing for him to have to be on his own for a while. People do their best thinking when they're alone, he said.

ROBERTA

I'm taking the spring term off. I'm behind on my own work as it is. And frankly I'm a little saturated with teaching . . .

GERALD

Roberta used to say photography is just a way of chasing shadows. You chase and chase until they're out of sight, then you try and find your way back, and if you're lucky there are points of interest along the way.

ROBERTA

You can overdo it, of course. Lose track of your life. Sometimes I like to quit early and go see some really cheesy movie. Just for fun.

THEA

It's weird, this thing that happened the other night. I caught my mom smoking. I got up to pee and I saw her in Dad's study, just standing at the window, puffing away. It was weird. I'd never seen her do it before. She'd take these really deep breaths and hold them in, then blow out the smoke. It was kind of scary to watch.

GERALD

Thanks for the charcoal and paper, by the way. They'll do nicely.

THEA

It was like she was somebody else, not my mom anymore, like if she looked up and saw me she wouldn't recognize me, either. But she didn't look up, so after a while I went back to bed. Only I couldn't fall asleep. I kept remembering the way her eyes looked behind the smoke, all half-shut and wet. I thought she was looking out the window, but now I wasn't sure. Because you could see *her* there, too, in the reflection. So I don't know. The smoke looked sort of blue in the light. Maybe she'd had more than one; maybe she'd been smoking for hours, maybe she'd smoked the whole pack. Even after she stubbed it out it just hung there around her shoulders. It was sort of pretty in a way. At least to me . . .

GERALD

Yes, well, I'm sorry, but I need a little time to myself now, okay? No offense. It's just that I'm anxious to get started. You can understand that, can't you . . .

THEA

I wonder if, you know, *he* ever saw her like that.

GERALD

. . . how anxious I am to get to work?

The Bachelor Party

Though we have been friends for many years now, I was not looking forward to Warren Pinsky's bachelor party. Anyone who has been to a bachelor party will understand why. Too long, too expensive, and too self-conscious, they invariably begin on a shrill note of forced gaiety and descend, as the evening progresses, into a meandering atonal fugue of sadness. Warren's party would be no different. For all his singular qualities and manias he was a conventional person, and so were his friends, many of whom were my friends as well. Together we had attended six or seven of these parties over the years—including, as it happened, both of Warren's previous ones. This would be his third. So I felt pretty certain I knew what to expect.

I myself had a quiet wedding, at a small inn near Gloucester, to which no one but immediate family was invited. In a sense this too had been conventional, though it did not strike me that way at the time. Neither did the marriage itself, while it lasted, or for that matter the divorce. We flatter ourselves that we are unique, even as the evidence mounts to the contrary. Take for example my relations with my daughter, who was off at the shore that summer with her mother and stepfather. She was going through a phase of refusing to speak to me on the phone. After some negotiation, she'd agreed to answer any questions I might have for her by mail. Her letters, in keeping with this spirit of formality, arrived every Friday, neatly written, immaculately folded, and succinct as haiku. I was reading over one of them, in fact, and trying to formulate a response, when the call came from Warren informing me of his impending marriage, and of the bachelor party that would precede it.

"It'll be great," he said. "Best ever."

"It's a terrible time for me, Warren. You have no idea."

"So you'll come, right?"

"The work's piled up. I've got half a dozen deadlines."

"It's a landmark event," he said. "The making of shared memories. This is what life is about, right?"

"I don't know what life is about."

"Well, I'm telling you."

The party would take place, I was informed, not on the Upper West Side, where I live, quite alone, and where Warren lived with each of his respective ex-wives until a few years ago, but in a condominium complex in Houston, Texas. The condo, he explained, belonged to his fiancée's parents. Bought as an investment during the boom years, it was now vacant, but as his fiancée was having a party at *their* apartment for the bachelorettes, the condo would have to do. His fiancée's name was Debbie Solomon. She was twenty-four years old and already halfway through medical school; perhaps that tells the story right there. I had never met the woman, but her voice—I could hear it in the background adding quippy commentary to our call—sounded smart and fresh and thoroughly assured, the voice of a young woman who has come through a comfortably limited set of trials with all her cleverness and ambitions intact. I may as well admit I found it heartbreaking to listen to. I could no longer remember what Warren, or I, or any of us, had sounded like at twenty-four, but I doubted if we had sounded like Debbie Solomon even then.

There was a thrilling sunset going on as I drove out of the airport, the oranges and violets heightened by emissions. The sky was still smeared like a dinner plate as I pulled up to the condo complex in my rental car. The front gate was locked. I had to work through an arduous series of mathematical codes before the metal door was persuaded to swing open, revealing the barren grid of the parking lot. I was looking for apartment 1102. Maybe I was not literally the only human being within sight, but it felt that way. Apparently the whole complex had gone bust. Taxiing past the rows of darkened windows and the iridescent geometry of the pool, I found a kind of ghost village on all sides, the dwellings silent and suspended under the elegiac halo of the sodium lights, as if an advertisement for some mediocre architectural firm that was no longer with us. Apartment 1102 was in the back, well within smelling range of an enormous Dumpster. The Dumpster, which loomed over the place like a landlord, had become a home away from home for the local cats. They eyed me speculatively, wondering what new manner of waste I represented, then went back to their business and left me to mine.

Stepping from the car I almost screamed from the heat. It was that bad. The cicadas were making their ferocious electrical noise, as though tuning up for Armageddon, and between them and the heat and the creepy uniform stillness of the complex around me, I went a little blank. It was as if I had forgotten everything there was to forget about myself, and would now have to relearn it all.

"You're late," said Warren cheerfully, when he opened the door.

He did not look well. Tall, balding, and gaunt, with question mark posture in the best of times, he seemed particularly tilted and stoop-shouldered to me that night. He stood there swaying in the doorway, holding a longneck bottle of Mexican beer in his left fist. The pinky of the right was engaged, urgently but methodically, in the dredging of wax from one ear. "It's already over," he said.

"Over? How can it be over?" I craned my neck to see whoever was in the room behind him, but no one was there, just some furniture of no particular color or taste and, behind it, the bare rough swirl of the stucco walls. "I thought you said eight o'clock. It's, what, eight-thirty now."

Warren shrugged, deferring to the relativity of time in general, and clinically examined the residue on his pinky.

"Half an hour? The whole thing's over in half an hour? What the hell kind of bachelor party is that?"

"A short one," he conceded. "Even shorter than usual."

"Where's everyone else?"

"That's the thing," he said, waving the beer like a magician's wand. "I sent them home."

"Home?"

"I don't blame you for being confused. It's perfectly natural under the circumstances."

"What circumstances? I have no idea what you're talking about."

"Perfectly natural," he assured me. "Even I'm confused. I had a little trouble just now in fact, finding the right words with the guys. They didn't quite get it."

"Well, let's call them back here and try again. Maybe you can find the words this time."

"You don't understand," he said. "I sent them *home.* Back where they came from—Chicago, Boston, D.C. They're halfway to the airport by now. You probably passed their cab on the road when you came in."

We were still in the doorway. At this point I wasn't feeling too great about my chances of being invited in.

"We were getting kind of worried about you," Warren said, almost accusingly. "Nobody wanted to leave until we knew where you were."

"I got held up."

"It happens." He offered a beneficent smile. "We all do the best we can."

For a moment we were silent, gauging the depths of the wall-to-wall carpet, and of each other's present mood. Warren and I were good friends, I considered, but not *this* good. Who's this good at thirty-nine? Who has the time? We were all operating by this point on diminished reserves.

"So Warren," I said conversationally, "what gives?"

"Gives? Nothing gives. Gives?" Now he turned and gave the parking lot behind me a challenging stare, as if it were my car that was affronting him. "I just decided I didn't want you guys around this time. That's all. I wanted a change. A clean start. Just this once. These things happen. I'm sorry if that sounds brutal."

"It doesn't sound brutal," I said.

"Selfish, then. I'm sorry if it sounds selfish."

"Don't forget stupid."

"You've got every right to be pissed," he said. "It was a late call, admittedly. I just decided a couple of hours ago, in fact. It wasn't easy." He glanced up at me quickly. "Look, I'm aware that for you guys this is not ideal. There's the time and expense, both considerable. I know this. Don't think I'm sending you home lightly."

"Warren," I said, "you're not sending me home."

"I'm not?" He looked genuinely surprised.

"It took me two hours to get to Newark. The plane was delayed on the runway for an hour and a half. My headphones didn't work. My seatmate was talkative and obese. I'm not turning around, is what I'm saying. I made arrangements for this."

"Arrangements." Warren clucked his tongue. "Tell me about it."

"Do you hear me, crazy person? I'm staying right here until after the wedding."

"Fine," he said, waving his beer apathetically in the direction of the street. "Whatever you say."

"I'm staying here, and all by myself, if I have to, I'm going to give you the best goddamn bachelor party you've ever had."

"Fine," he said again.

"You want a clean start, you'll get a clean start. A clean start, a great wedding, and a marriage that lasts forever."

"Why not," he said. "Stranger things have happened."

"Exactly."

"Maybe it's good," he said, suddenly thoughtful. "That you're here, I mean. Maybe that's a good thing."

"Of course it is."

"You can't cut off all ties to the past. That's no way to live."

"If I agree with you, will you let me in the house? And maybe also pour me a humongous scotch?"

He shook his head. "I sent the booze home with the guys. Also the food. It was their idea, actually. It seemed to make them a little less surly about everything."

"What about my surliness?"

"I could get some grass," he offered. "I know a guy."

"I don't want grass."

"Since when?"

"I don't know. Yesterday. My shrink's against it. Makes me too passive, he says."

"I saw a shrink for a while," Warren reflected. "He said my problem was I didn't dress well enough. I ever tell you this?"

"Hundreds of times."

The doorbell chimed, one of those long melodious windsongs designed to foster tranquility in the face of unexpected company. Warren cocked his head, suspicious. He appeared to be gathering his long limbs for imminent flight. "You get it," he said.

I knew who it would be. Steve, Big Frank, Mitchell Fine, the whole group—they'd realized, halfway to the airport, that Warren wasn't serious, that this was only another of the failed, arbitrary whims that comprised his existence. But it wasn't them. The person it was I had never met before. Short, pointy-featured, dressed in ripped jeans and a black teeshirt, his dark hair pulled back into a frizzy three-inch ponytail, he could not have been over seventeen. He had round, cartoonlike biceps that could only have come from the gym, and perhaps because of the effort they'd cost him he seemed a little tired. His eyes were narrow and listless. They nodded in and out of the shadows that fell from the porch light as if he were listening to some desultory piece of music. I stuck out my hand, and he sized it up without interest and stepped forward into the apartment. His face, I could see now, was one big bruise. Acne and stubble wheeled angrily across his cheeks, like a map of that weird far-flung cosmos called adolescence.

"You must be here for the bachelor party," I said.

"You a friend of Warren?"

"Right," I said.

"Cool."

We let things rest on that note for a while, and headed side by side into the living room. It was deserted.

"Am I, like, late? Where is everybody?"

"You'll have to talk to Warren about that."

"Okay, sure. Only where's he at?"

"Probably hiding in the bathroom," I said.

"I do that."

"He thought you were his old friends," I explained.

"Hey, I hardly know the guy. Only met him that one time. Passover, I think. Whoa boy, did he piss off my old man. Only one who came in jeans, except for me."

I went off to the kitchen to fetch us some beers, and to ponder the mysterious power of the Jewish holidays, which had their origins in miracles, like the parting of seas and the onslaught of plagues, and which had somehow managed to engineer an alliance between the podiatrist Warren Pinsky and this little acidhead from the wrestling team who was casing the living room. Baruch Ha'Shem!

"Christ," Warren said. "It's Kenny."

"Hey." Kenny looked up from *TV Guide,* blinked, and rose uncertainly in greeting. "What's up, Bro?"

"Kenny, you know what? I completely forgot you were coming."

"That's okay. I'm sure you got a lot on your mind, the wedding and all. Your buddy here let me in."

At this point Warren turned to me—accusingly, I thought—and explained, "Kenny is Debbie's little brother. He flew in from Philly this morning. I forgot all about it."

"You forgot a lot of things."

"Don't be nasty. You're now officially my only friend. Etiquette dictates that you be supportive."

Kenny was looking over his beer from Warren to me and back again, nodding in a kind of generalized agreement with the direction of our exchange. "I never been to one of these bachelor things," he said. "What're we supposed to do, party or something, just the guys?"

"Something like that," Warren said.

"Cool. Got any tunes?"

"There's no stereo."

"Any drugs?"

"Nope."

"That TV get cable?"

Warren shook his head.

"Oh, hey, I get it," Kenny said, taking it all in stride. "Some kind of zen thing, right? We don't do anything. We just, you know, let it flow."

"Right," said Warren thoughtfully. "Let it flow."

"We'll just do nothing. *Commune.*"

"Right." Warren fingered his chin as if the idea had made it itchy. Then he drained the last of his beer. I drained the last of mine. Kenny drained the last of his. Then, in no particular hurry, we all went into the kitchen and brought back several more.

"You know," Warren said, falling into a mood I recognized at once from other parties, other weddings, "maybe the kid's right."

"About what?"

"Maybe the problem with these things is we go about them the wrong way. We're too programmed, too goal-oriented. We've lost track of the process. I mean, we didn't have these stupid institutional hangups back in '69."

"We were twelve in '69."

"Exactly. Kids, they're closer to pure knowledge. Pure instinct. Remember *Childhood's End*?"

"No. Remember *Lord of the Flies*?"

"Listen," he said. "This kid Kenny, he's a *savant* of sorts, Debbie tells me. Computer games, physics, SATs through the roof. He says let it flow. This to me sounds like good advice."

Inside every foot doctor is a latent guru, slouching eastward to be born. And inside the rest of us, maybe he's there too, a chubby little man with his legs crossed, speaking calmly of all that we're helpless to control. Cleanse your mind, the man tells us.

Shut off the distractions and listen. All our troubles arise from our inability to sit still in a quiet room . . .

"Fine," I said. "Let it flow."

And so we did. We arranged ourselves on the white carpet in such a way that we were able to extend ourselves without touching, and assumed what we all agreed was the most meditative posture we knew of—that is, lying down. Immediately Kenny Solomon gave out with a soft but audible belch. "Sorry," he said.

"Work on your breathing," called Warren, who'd done some yoga at some point, along with everything else. "Breathing is the key."

Indeed, this proved true. The more I worked on my breathing, the more key it seemed. I focused on it my full attention, or half of it anyway—the other half tracking, as if against my will, the irregularities on the stucco ceiling overhead—and in time, as I concentrated on them both, on my breathing and on the ceiling, both of these things came to seem related to each other, or at least related through me, part of some good soundless energy that was working through us all, the whole great revolving world and all its wayward bachelors. And though it was getting sort of cold on the floor, and the carpet smelled faintly of mold, I tuned that out as best I could. My skin under the overhead light felt as soft and pliant as a rose petal. It practically tingled. The sensation was nothing like what I had experienced at any of Warren's previous bachelor parties.

Then, like a gunshot, came a ripping adenoidal snore across the room. Kenny Solomon was curled into a ball, asleep. Watching him from several feet away, dolorously sipping another beer, sat Warren Pinsky. "He's good," he said. "He's very good."

"What about you?"

"Can't get the breathing right. I'm a little rusty."

"So what now, Gregorian chants?"

"Don't make fun. The concept is sound. You didn't seem to be having such a bad time over there."

To this I said nothing.

"Maybe we should go for a drive. Go down to Galveston and walk on the beach, talk over the big questions. How's that sound?"

I agreed it was a good idea. Nonetheless neither of us moved. We drank our beers, somewhat reflectively, and sat there listening to the sounds that the cats made in the Dumpster outside, their back-and-forth choreography of desire and avoidance. Probably half an hour passed before we roused ourselves to go. "What about Kenny?" Warren asked as we moved toward the door.

"Let him sleep."

"He'll wake up and we won't be here. He may flip out. He's a sensitive kid."

This wasn't the word I'd have used, exactly, but what did I know? Sensitivity is as elusive and protean in its forms, I suppose, as anything else. And when Warren shook him awake, Kenny Solomon did look pleasantly surprised, as if his sleep had borne him to a lonely place and then at the critical moment returned him to us, our team of men. His eyes, reddened and small, shone moistly. Rising from the floor, he pulled the rubber band from his ponytail in one fluid motion and shook out his lank brown hair. For a second he was almost handsome.

"Cool," he said, upon being informed of the flow's new direction. "Let's cruise."

Outside the night was balmy and starless. The Gulf breeze carried off the smell of the Dumpster, and made it possible to resist the urge to retreat to the air-conditioned condo at once. "You've got a flat," Warren said, indicating one of my rear tires.

"You're kidding."

"No, it's very flat. Look."

"Flat," young Kenny put in. "Absolutely."

We stared at it for a while. I don't know why. Perhaps we were still adjusting to the outdoors, or else we thought there was a chance that the flat would disobey the laws of physics as they applied to rental cars, and assume its proper shape. This seemed to be an evening for magical thinking. "Let's take yours," I said. "Where is it?"

"I got dropped off," Warren said.

"Me too," said Kenny.

"Well, we'll take a train then."

"Train?" Warren laughed. "There is no train. This is the Sun Belt. There's only cars and pickup trucks with bumper stickers about Jesus."

"What about buses? You must have buses."

"There may be buses, I'm not sure. Nobody I know has ever ridden one. Philosophically speaking, if you've never ridden a bus, can they be said to exist? Anyway, even if they do they won't take us to Galveston. It's fifty miles."

"We'll walk," declared Kenny Solomon. He jerked his head toward the skyline in the distance. "Do us good."

"Fifty *miles*?"

"No, hey, I just mean, let's just, like, *walk.* You know? See the sights."

Warren looked in my direction hopefully. "The flow," he reminded me.

Suddenly the evening—the whole summer—caught up with me in full. "Fuck the flow," I said.

"Fuck the flow?" Kenny Solomon giggled. "Righteous."

"I've had the flow up to here. I'm flowed out."

"Now now." Warren laid a hand on my shoulder. "This is my party, don't forget. A walk might feel good. We can just stroll around the neighborhood here and pretend we're on a beautiful beach."

It was no easy thing, surrounded by that low malignant riot of strip malls and streetlights, to pretend we were on a beautiful beach, but by this point in the evening I no longer cared. We wandered through the complex next to ours, and then the one next to that, searching in vain for a sidewalk that would take us to the avenue a few blocks away, which we could hear from the cars whooshing by, but not see. The breeze worked its way around us, clinging to our clothes. Kenny Solomon walked in front, his uselessly muscled arms swinging like Popeye's as he charted a path through the maze of developments. He was kicking rocks with his high-tops and humming a tune I didn't recognize.

"Mahler," said Warren. "He's humming Mahler."

"You know, I may be nuts," I said, "but I sort of like that kid."

"Me too. He's going to be my brother-in-law in a couple of days. How's that for strange?"

"No stranger than anything else."

Warren nodded. He looked over his shoulder for something in the distance, but couldn't seem to find it. "Third time's a charm. That's what they say."

"Who?"

"How should I know? The other guys who've gotten married three times, probably."

"They must know what they're talking about, then."

"I'm just a silly, immature jerk, aren't I? Tell me the truth."

"Are these the big questions? Is that what we're doing now?"

"The depressing fact is," Warren went on, "I still believe in it. I still believe in everything."

"That's not depressing."

"Oh yes it is," he said.

"Does Debbie believe in everything?"

"What's not to believe in? She's twenty-four, for christ's sake."

"So it's a match. That's not depressing."

"Yes it is. Because she's going to change one day, and I still haven't."

I thought of my daughter's letters, back on my desk, those very secular and guarded documents. Nothing like the garrulous child I used to carry on my shoulders through the park. But it occurred to me that perhaps the line between believing in everything and believing in nothing was a fine one, so fine it might not even exist. Perhaps we never cross it, or perhaps we cross it all the time without knowing. And if so, then I was glad to be the one down here with Warren, the only friend, past or present, enduring this alternately hopeful and depressing party of his.

A phrase of music floated toward us, borne up by the breeze. Warren heard it too. He slowed down to listen, patting his bald spot in an experimental way I recognized—he'd been doing it, I thought, since before he *had* a bald spot—and at the sight of it I felt rising in me a large, formless, thoroughly mingled emotion that was by a kind of spiritual squatters' rights our mutual property, something I wanted to put into words, even if I'd said it before at his first bachelor party, or his second . . . but before I could quite get it all assembled we were brought up short by Kenny Solomon's loud, portentous gasp. "What the fuck is *that*?"

"That," Warren said, "is the Astrodome." And so it was. In his voice was an inflection of proud surprise, and also, who knows, a measure of wonder.

"Look, man, it's all lit up," Kenny said. "Like a spaceship."

"Or a wedding cake," I said.

"Yow."

We could hear organ music coming from inside, and a few seconds later, the dull tumescent roar of a crowd. They were playing ball.

"Let's check it out," said Kenny.

"It's late. The game'll be almost over."

"So what? I hate baseball anyway. I just want to see."

"Me too," piped in Warren.

"You? You never went to a baseball game in your life."

But it was the flow again, I could see that, there was no fighting it. We made our way toward that dome of light, which hovered over the gray acreage of the parking lot like an invitation to dream, and we paid our money and went inside. I don't know what inning it was. All I remember is the wave of sound that greeted us when we came off the ramp, and the discovery of that luminous green field below. As we descended toward our seats, the arena seemed to open itself to us, to breathe and spread and enfold us like a lover. People in bright hats handed us food and drinks; we accepted these graciously. We accepted everything that happened. It was easy. When you accept everything, nothing by itself can disturb your equilibrium, and so perhaps that was why we were able to lose ourselves, despite our lousy seats and our general indifference to sports, in the last innings of a lopsided game of no special merit or relevance. At the plate, the Astros in their candy-stripe uniforms were losing badly. We didn't know their names, but we cheered them on anyway, those young men down there in their poised, impeccable isolation, those losers—and our voices mingled with those of the others until they were unrecognizable to us.

Then someone slashed a grounder through the hole.

Immediately a kind of sonic boom issued from the scoreboard, and we were on our feet.

"I'm getting married!" screamed Warren Pinksy in the direction of the field.

The crowd roared.

Adult Education

Sylvia I say very frankly this will not do.

Sylvia nodding pats her stomach.

Sylvia I say this will not do. I am not ready. I have an idea in my head I say and this idea is not so much an idea but a kind of vision, a vision concerning readiness. I have this idea that concerns and surrounds readiness like a glove but the problem Sylvia as I see it is that without the hard defining hand of readiness inside it the idea is limp and of no use whatever when it comes to carrying things.

Sylvia smiles dreamily, munches a cracker.

The thing is Sylvia that the world is equipped in a certain way, or rather people are equipped in a certain way, that is people have different kinds of equipment that ready them for different kinds of work, and these differences of equipment account for certain differences in schedules and timing when it comes to the actualizing of certain inchoate needs, if you will, and these needs as such are—

Sweetie, Sylvia says, I'm going to lie down now.

—neither good nor bad in any valuative way, but simply

exist, like rocks and trees, like . . . like rocks and trees. Let's keep things plain, let's keep things solid, because Plato notwithstanding we live in a world of solid objects Sylvia after all, and against these solid objects our various whims and yearnings are really not very substantial when you examine them closely, not very—

Whims, says Sylvia. Ha. This is not whims.

I know Sylvia I know I say but see that's my point that's exactly my . . . it's so good and typical of you to discover it. You are right that this is not whims. This is a solid object with some fluids in it, one that will eventually become more and more solid despite having more and more fluids in it, and pretty soon according to what I have heard from other people all these solids and fluids are going to drive us right out of this life of ours that's been going so well without them.

It hasn't been going so well says Sylvia. If you knew anything you'd know it hasn't been going so well. What makes you think it's been going so well?

You have done it again Sylvia I say. You have put the finger of meaning right on the very throbbing pulse of the problem. Because it hasn't been going so well has it? We have issues among us and between us, and these issues are lingering and penetrant, like most issues, and cannot be ignored, and therefore clearly the last thing we need, the last thing that would be advisory under the circumstances, that is given the expanding network of pressures we operate under and the frail not to say delicate state of our emotional health—

Expanding says Sylvia. I'll show you expanding.

—or at least *my* emotional health, such as it is Sylvia such as it is. This emotional health of mine, how do I say this? This emotional health of mine is an extremely small and unseaworthy metaphoric boat that is presently getting pounded by a very strong metaphoric wind, and right now, before it sails off into the black distance or capsizes forever, I would like to offer a few words just for the record by way of eulogy. Ladies and gentlemen, we were close once, my emotional health and I. Frequently we went out together back in our youth, drank at bars together and so forth, long nights studded like stars with possibilities, we were allies the two of us in the hectic bloody wars of existence and as happens in combat we grew close. The melancholy fact is that I miss my emotional health. It was never very sturdy but it deserved a longer life. It may be sentimental of me, but the thought of it out there now, pale, bloated, pecked by circling fowl, losing the last of its shape to the blind currents, this makes me want to cry out loud. This makes me want to *act*.

Good says Sylvia. Would you mind very much acting your way over to the popcorn?

Fine I say. But it was your friend too Sylvia once, I know it was. I beg you search your heart for a sign of it, some small flicker of this thing you once prized but apparently prize no longer. I beg—

Let's watch the news says Sylvia. She plumps a pillow and sticks it behind her back. Reaches for the popcorn.

—you, please before it's too late, search inside yourself. What do you see when you search inside yourself Sylvia.

You saw it too says Sylvia. At the doctor's.

That wasn't me Sylvia I say. That wasn't me. That was only this construction that wears my name. That was only this puppet of cartilage and bone that attends to the world while the real me cowers in dark rooms, wondering when the movie is going to start. I have no idea at all Sylvia what doctor you're talking about. What doctor? I haven't been to a doctor, oh, in a long, a long—

Don't be silly she says. We looked at it together. You squeezed my hand.

No. That was not me. That was only the puppet and his puppet reflex. It had nothing *intentional* in it. For intention to register Sylvia there must be a seedling of conscious forethought involved, there must be—

You cried she says.

Same thing. The exact same phenomenon I say. I rest my case.

Look she says and points to the frenzied screen. Famine. War. She puts the popcorn down and holds her stomach as if someone very big has entered the room and threatened to hurt her. Volcanic lava she says.

Volcanic lava?

Red and flowing she says.

Red and flowing?

Red and flowing.

Sylvia I fail to understand—

Quite all right she says. Failure is forgivable.

It is?

Understanding comes later she says after the fact. One regards the object and one is simultaneously seized by something blind and thirsty inside oneself and then very slowly this seizure yields an oblique recognition of connection between the object and oneself and in this way is the ineffable sublime approached.

Sylvia I say where did you learn to talk like this all of a sudden?

Adult education she says.

Sylvia I say come to bed now and make this planet spin. Bring all the attendant blindness and thirst you can muster.

Not now she says. I'm a little nauseous. You're going to have to carry me.

Okay. I am going to have to carry you.

Just a few steps she says.

Nothing. Hardly measurable.

You're sweating she says.

Not me.

Beads of sweat. Your brow is full of them.

A natural process. Nothing to worry about.

Look she says I can play connect the dots on your head.

A small irritation, Sylvia, under the circumstances.

Are we almost there?

Almost I say.

And when we arrive? What then?

I don't know.

Will you carry me back?

I don't know if I'll have the strength.

I know you don't know she says. Just say you will.

I don't see the point of saying I will I say when I don't know if I will.

I know you don't know she says.

Well if you know I don't know then it stands to reason—

Stands shmands she says. Say you will.

Of course I'll say it I say.

You will she says.

I will.

Oscillations

The doctor says I can go home now.

He sits in his leather chair, hands folded over his waist, his long, hairless fingers twined into a net. Dr. Kai is a subtle and brilliant man; even the way he sits conveys a pedagogical message. In the fit of his hands one can read a lesson of organic unity. The body, as they say here at the institute, is subtle but not mean. Inside each one of us, laid out like a grid, is a network of complementary anatomical, psychological, hormonal, and linguistic structures, which in turn allow us to function—I'm paraphrasing Dr. Kai here—within a larger social system made up of its own equivalent and parallel structures, and somewhere within this mesh of inner grid and outer grid lie those gray, baggy pockets of indeterminacy which we call human behavior. My own behavior has been *very* gray; I'll be the first to concede that. But now, thanks to Dr. Kai, the necessary adjustments have been made, and I must return home.

It is time, he says.

The doctor has sympathetic rhythms; I follow them easily. His voice, deep and sonorous as a cello, underscores the melody of his meaning. Together we have established a language community of breadth and suppleness, one that permits us to communicate easily, without the sort of problems I for one fell prey to beyond the walls of the institute. Perhaps Kai has difficulties in that sphere too. Who knows what his domestic life is like? There are no photos on his desk of children or a wife; he could for all I know be a solitary, an onanist. There is something blurry and evasive at the center of his features. He is one of those young men who has both middle-aged looks—stolid, blandly handsome, grave with unseen responsibilities—and middle-aged habits. He wears cardigan vests. He's exceptionally well groomed. He keeps trim by playing hours of handball with Dr. Bloom in the institute gym. His hair is black and thick, with a small unruly wave over the left temple which he is not above fondling absently during our sessions, provided his hands are not otherwise engaged, as they are now, with each other, in their immaculate fold.

He cocks his head and scrutinizes me carefully. "Are you feeling all right, Mr. Statler?"

I nod.

"Please," he says. "If you would like to respond, I request it be verbally."

I indulge in a bit more nodding.

"Yes would be sufficient. A good, hearty yes."

I am content for the moment to listen to his voice, that remarkable instrument. Even now, with its shadow of impatience, it is attended by an aura, a fuzzy little corona of benevolent light.

"Mr. Statler, I am disappointed. I do not believe your behavior is sincere. I believe quite frankly that you are being either petulant or dishonest. Is it really so traumatic to return home? Have you not spent much of your time here anticipating just such an eventuality?"

I nod in a manner which might superficially resemble my

previous nods, but which I'm confident Dr. Kai, with all his fine training, will decode as a signal of agreement.

Possibly I'm wrong, however. Kai frowns, his eyes narrowing into slits. "We had hoped, Mr. Statler, that your treatment would have made such behavior obsolete. Perhaps our feedback procedures need review. Perhaps we are guilty of overestimating your progress. It seems more likely, however, in my opinion, that you are deliberately subverting your own achievements, and ours too, at a crucial hour. You are angry with us. With me. It is the kind of separation anxiety we see in children. Why not admit this to be so?"

Very well, I say. *You're right. You're right. You're right.*

"Still not talking?" Dr. Kai shakes his head.

I thought I was *talking.*

"Ah well," he sighs. "Perhaps later. There is still a little time."

Though you would never guess it to look at me now, I was not particularly eager to come to the institute. In fact I resisted the idea when it was first put to me by my psychiatrist, Irwin Roud. I had already seen several doctors at that point. I had already been run like a lab rat through a maze of tests. None had been conclusive, or even revealing. The last specialist on my list, pleading a full appointment book, had sent me to Irwin Roud, well known in our city for both his acuity and his fee structure. I surrendered my credit card and took up occupancy on his leather couch. "Tell me about your condition," Roud said. And I did. Of course it took a while, because of my condition.

It is difficult to speak of my condition in layman's terms, but I'll try. Simply put, I had developed a problem with speech. The chains had fallen off the gears of my verbal motor mechanisms. It was not a stutter per se. Not even close to a stutter. This was more like a stammer—a seething, arrhythmic hyper-fluency, which, as it ran its wobbly course, began to noisily degenerate, the vowels blurring, the consonants crumpling at the edges, until all recognizable meaning was lost, and what remained was a kind of guttural fragmented hacking for which no dictionary existed. It was an alarming development in my life. Increasingly I would find, at moments of high emotion—an argument with my son, for example, or a stressful meeting at the firm, or while giving instructions to our gross, half-witted contractor about the expansion of the house—that at a certain point in the conversation the other party was staring at me with fixed bewilderment, as if I were no longer a sentient person but a babbling, incomprehensible animal. Who could blame them? I *was* babbling. I *was* incomprehensible. Except I didn't know it. For in my own ears I sounded as I always had, a bit wordy, a bit run-on, perhaps, but perfectly, horribly normal.

Of course it is common among victims of illness to seek a cause, a trigger, a local branch office of this formless, general affliction in which to register a complaint, and I was no different. But there *was* no cause. I had a good job, a stable marriage, and a reliable therapist. I had not met Jesus in the airport, had not been struck by lightning in the backyard, had not even been particularly depressed, so far as I was aware, about the onset of middle age. Irwin Roud at the age of forty-four bought a convertible Saab at full price and put three thousand dollars worth of silver on his teeth. Apparently he had always felt self-conscious about the gaps, the buckled tilting. As for me, I already owned a Saab. My life, like my teeth, had been well-braced to start with; there were no prominent gaps, and very few buckles. Though that was beginning to change.

First there was some damage done at our Thanksgiving dinner, the nature of which I'd rather not go into at the moment. Then, at the office, after weeks of my calls being rerouted behind my back to other agents, I was granted a month of unpaid and unrequested leave. Around this time, the tension with Linda became more pronounced, as tension so often does. I made my first visit to Irwin Roud to appease her. His exam turned up nothing. Then I tried two more specialists. Privately I thought, this is stress, nothing more; I'll get over this on my own. My failure to do so resulted in the debacle of the Tabacks' twentieth anniversary party, where I delivered what I understand now to be, in retrospect, a rather meandering and controversial toast. So I went back to Irwin Roud, who sent me to the institute, where an interview with the Admissions Team was arranged.

The institute was about an hour and a half up the coast, in a cluster of undistinguished office buildings of the kind seen everywhere nowadays and known, oxymoronically, as the industrial park. It was sparsely but carefully landscaped, all but windowless from the outside. I parked in a visitor space and locked the car up tight. The glass doors whooshed open with a sigh. Immediately I was enveloped by a beam of light so strong it made the walls and corridors around me, and the carpet below my feet, glow like an x-ray. I looked up to discover an enormous domed skylight, fracturing the sun's illuminations and then redistributing them in what seemed, gazing upward, an infinitely calmer, shapelier, more generous way. Young people in lab coats and clogs hustled around me energetically, as though engaged in the Lord's own errands. I wrote my name in the reception log and sat on one of the sofas to await my interview. The quiet intensity of the building's rhythms, the hum of its constituent parts, was so hypnotic and persuasive it made you want to lie down.

But I didn't, of course. I chose a *National Geographic* from the well-stocked rack and looked it over. Sea turtles, toucans, wildebeests, Arctic explorations . . . every page seemed like an advertisement for this marvelous, variegated world of ours, so intricately patterned in color and light. I should get back, I thought. Nature after all was full of strange, exotic adaptations, much stranger and more exotic than my own. Let it run its course.

But even as I rose to leave the receptionist was waving me in for my interview.

I entered a small, tidy office. Because of the many bookshelves crammed with texts and journals, there was space enough for only two chairs and a desk, behind which sat a man whose name I didn't know. He had a file open before him; when I came in he glanced at it once reluctantly, and then turned to me. "Please sit down."

He had a pleasant if inexpressive face and a disarming manner. He was younger than I was and that bothered me somewhat, but I could see a fine, lucid intelligence in his eyes.

"You must be very confused," the doctor said.

I nodded.

"How lonely it must be, having your condition. How baffling and troublesome and unfair. You must be thinking to yourself, why me?"

I bowed my head silently in acknowledgment.

"The isolation must be terrible. The futility. There's nothing worse, is there, Mr. Statler, than to be locked up in yourself, unable to find the key."

Like most educated people, I am conversant with the basic tenets of the therapeutic relationship, issues of transference and countertransference and so forth, so I do not want to make too much of the fact that I wished with all my heart to embrace the man, to clamber up onto his trim, elegant lap and remain there until I was healed.

"Here you are," he said, "a perfectly healthy individual, living a perfectly normal life. A husband and a father. An active member of your professional and community associations. Athletically vigorous. According to Dr. Roud, you're quite a tennis player. Though your serve—" he glanced down at the file, "yes, your serve, he finds relevant to mention, is somewhat erratic."

I shrug. There's no denying it.

"And yet something appears to be slightly off. Something more serious. I wonder, Mr. Statler, if you'd be willing to just describe to me, in your own words, what you think is wrong. Will you do that?"

And so I did. I told him everything, emptied out the whole reservoir. It felt, in its way, rather cleansing, like a ritualized purge or insomniacal confession, and by the time I was done I was sweating heavily and could feel a sticky accumulation at the corners of my mouth which I knew to be saliva. The doctor listened calmly, taking in the movements of my hands and feet, the wriggling of my backside on the narrow chair. Even when I was finished he continued to listen. Even when I leaned back, exhausted and despairing, he remained attentive, even absorbed, though of course I knew he had not understood a word.

"Well," he said. "That was quite a speech, wasn't it?"

I waved my wrist dispiritedly.

"I believe," he said, "we should start treatment immediately."

And so we did.

"The mechanism of voluntary activity in our species," he explained, after the first round of tests, "is of a feedback nature. Accordingly, we search for the characteristics of breakdown which feedback mechanisms exhibit when they are overloaded. In your case, Mr. Statler, we find an oscillation in the goal-seeking process of speech which appears only when that process is actively invoked."

I nod dreamily. His words in all truth are difficult to follow. Instead I concentrate on the musical patterns of his voice, the slow undulations.

"The term we employ for a condition like yours is an *intention tremor.* This is roughly a variant of the palsied tremor. Think of how an old person's hand shakes when he cannot reach a desired object. Now, typically the source of this tremor lies within the subassemblies of neurons in the cerebellum. But our tests in your case point elsewhere. They suggest we are dealing with an involuted voluntary response. In any event our procedure is clear: we must reduce in you the level of feedback associated with the act of constructing language. Do you understand?"

I shake my head.

"What I am saying is that your ability to process phonetic and semantic information is not organically impaired. You are for example able to understand what I am saying right now, are you not?"

I nod.

"In the same way you are able, phonetically, to communicate, to be understood. You have simply chosen, on some unconscious level, not to. This is the oscillation of semantic intent we must correct."

I take out my pen and paper, write down a question, and hand it across to Dr. Kai.

"That doesn't concern us," he says. "We are not a psychoanalytic facility. We are research scientists in the area of behavior. Questions of motivation, I think, are best reserved for later. After you have healed."

He says this so forcefully that I am vaguely ashamed of myself for raising the issue. Perhaps he is angry with me. It's difficult to be sure. I may not be receiving his full semantic intent. One never does, according to Dr. Kai. It is a physical law. We do not receive all the information that is sent in our direction. There is some dissipation of quality along the way. Perhaps my tremor is simply an acceleration of this trend, and that is why I have so much trouble being understood. I console myself with precedents: Moses, Aristotle, Virgil. Casey Stengel. Great minds are as notable for their lags and blank spaces as they are for their illuminations. Only mine, I know, is not a great mind. It is merely an average one, plagued with worry and shadowed by regret, like that of most people.

Dr. Kai looks pointedly at his watch. We are overdue at the lab.

In the beginning, I am connected by wires to the Vocoder. To describe the workings of that device is beyond my powers, but my understanding is that the Vocoder somehow streamlines auditory signals, narrowing verbal frequencies so that what actually gets transmitted, after being processed by the machine, is an agreeable, linear hum—the sound of one's own words coming back in layered bands of transmission, pleasant, simple, and intelligible, a distillation of all that is impure. I get the hang of it pretty quickly. Indeed, it isn't hard. I have always been a quick study, and I have little else to do but interact with the machine.

Still, the results are better than any of us expected. After a few weeks of daily Vocoder repetitions, my tremor begins to recede. Dr. Kai and his colleague Dr. Bloom express cautious optimism about my prospects. It will make for an excellent article, in any case. They leave the lab murmuring of funding proposals, deadlines. I return to my room, spread out on the narrow cot, and write my daily letter to Linda.

We encounter a small setback in the fifth week of treatment. I am in Kai's office, working with the machine, when I look up to find that snow is falling outside the window, piling onto the branches of the maple trees and the hoods of the cars. While I have been away, the world, I realize, has gone on turning without me. If I don't finish my treatment soon my Christmas will be spent alone.

As if in response to this thought, Bloom walks in and declares that in light of my rapid progress he would like to try a bold new experiment. He suggests that I initiate a phone conversation with a friend or acquaintance, someone who can be counted on for warmth but will not cause me undue stress. My wife and children are off-limits; otherwise it's up to me. The phone, he explains, will of itself narrow the range of transmission, though I may of course experience certain distortions and impurities on the line.

Kai looks reluctant. He asks Bloom if he has done a literature search. Bloom says no, he's just arrived at the idea. "We'll write it up afterwards," he says. "That will be the literature."

Kai weighs the prospect for a moment, gazing off at the clouds hanging leaden over the commercial strip in the distance. "What do you think?" he asks me.

If I pull this off to everyone's satisfaction, I say, *can I go home soon?*

The doctors confer for a moment, and then agree.

Okay then. I choose my brother William.

"Brother?" Bloom looks unhappy about this. He leans over to confer again with Dr. Kai.

William, I explain, is ten years older, and because of our disparity in age we have never been close. He lives in Seattle, where he operates a modest steakhouse and lives with a pretty, rather low-affect piano tuner named Ruth. I have only met Ruth once, at my mother's funeral, and we did not impress each other, so I have been more than content over the years to keep my distance.

This has not been hard. She and William, as a concession to some faded ideal of bohemianism, have never married, so anniversaries are not a problem, and I'm not sure she even celebrates Christmas. Now William and I talk on the phone about twice a year, on our respective birthdays. When we hang up we are always glad to have spoken and never sorry that we live on opposite coasts. Plus, I add, William knows nothing of my condition.

Dr. Kai seems convinced. He agrees that William is an excellent choice.

Bloom retreats to the adjoining room, where he will watch from behind the two-way mirror and monitor the video camera. Kai remains. Impassively he watches me dial William's number. It is ten in the morning here, which means, I realize too late, only seven in Seattle. But the connection has already gone through.

There is a soft crackle on the line, like sparks from a contained fire, and what happens next I am not prepared for: Ruth answers. I am momentarily struck dumb, both by surprise and by the jagged, querulous quality of her voice. "Who's this?" she asks several times. "Who *is* this?"

I tell her who it is in what seems to me the clearest imaginable way.

"What? Listen, can you speak up?" I am reminded of the sound of a lawn mower laboring over a stand of wet, chunky weeds. "I can't hardly hear you."

I repeat myself, loudly, more than once.

Dr. Kai leans forward, his expression guarded, opaque. At least I find it so. It is difficult to concentrate all of a sudden, what with all the phone noise, the washy waves of static and interference, and my brother's not-quite-wife's weary, abrasive voice rattling around in my ear.

I ask for William. I ask for William several times. Ruth, for her part, continues to ask who I am. It's hopeless. Our input signals are not attuned, our rhythms remain unsympathetic. We go on this way for another minute, flailing like teenagers on a dance floor, until I drop the phone and begin to sob. Ruth's voice continues to leak from the receiver, a tinny trickle from an angry distant sea.

"There, there," says Dr. Kai, patting my shoulder. It is a conventional, even predictable gesture; perhaps that is why it moves me so deeply. "One must endure many frustrations on the long road to knowledge. Science teaches us this truth every day."

Science! Don't talk to me of science!

"Communication," he shrugs. "A complex art. So many signals. It is a wonder we have even the success that we do. In fact it's counterintuitive. Your affliction, Mr. Statler, should be not the exception but the rule."

Great! Very comforting!

"Tomorrow we will take a new direction. I believe it will yield great benefits. Soon, you'll see, the memory of today will be just a harmless residue of neurons in the cerebellum."

And so I miss Christmas, and instead am forced to begin a new course of treatment, Play Analog Therapy, an approach I find singularly humiliating. PAT sessions are held in a carpeted lounge down in the basement, one that's padded with wrestling mats and smells faintly but distinctly of human waste. The air is cool and moldy. The walls rumble from the dryers in the laundry room nearby. This is the domain of our three toddlers—Babe, Kid, and Shorty—whom Dr. Bloom assumed guardianship over, under god knows what auspices, from the state orphanage. Other people's children are never quite so appealing as our own, I realize that, and Babe, Kid, and Shorty are doubtless cute in their way; still, it must be said, the hours that we spend together are something of a trial.

Imagine a day care center in Hell, and you have an approximation of PAT. I am required to interact with the children for several hours a day, only leaving when they take their afternoon naps. Essentially what we do together, the four of us, is play. The lounge is generously equipped with toys and games and puzzles, and because I am, after all, a grown man, I am able to master them easily and concentrate upon my *real* task, which is to practice the most elementary forms of communication in a low-pressure environment. The idea is to express myself in simple, preliterate sounds: moans and gurgles, onomatopoetic syllables, occasional shrieks, and so forth. As an infant, let me just say, I am not particularly adorable. I discover I have a tendency to whine, and to make hostile growling noises through my molars when crossed. Shorty, particularly, gets on my nerves, with his capacious drooling, though Babe and Kid frequently irritate me as well.

One morning late in January I throw a bit of a tantrum. Babe has broken my favorite truck and is busy sticking its fragments under his shirt, as if to hide the damage. Kid has wet himself and this always occasions a lot of noise. And then Shorty, for no earthly reason, crawls up my back and bites down hard on the fleshy part of my ear. It is a mean thing to do and I cry out in anger and pain, flinging him backwards against the wall with a violent movement of my arm. Now he's crying too. Good. Why should I be the only one?

So there we are, the three of us crying from our respective positions on the wrestling mats, the videocamera high on the wall recording it for posterity, and Dr. Kai, I know, sitting on the opposite side of the two-way mirror, jotting down notes for his latest article, when suddenly it occurs to me with great lucidity and force that I want very much to die.

"*Want!*" I hear myself cry. "*Die!*"

Dr. Kai pokes his head into the room. "Did you say something, Mr. Statler?"

"*Want!*"

He scrunches up his forehead, which is normally quite smooth. "Again?"

"*Want . . .*" I gurgle. Now Shorty and Kid are gurgling too. Babe, a slow learner, has just begun to cry.

"Louder please, Mr. Statler."

"*Want! Want!*"

Kai scratches the mole on his cheek with a trembling index finger. "Continue," he says. "Want what?"

"*Want!*"

He studies me quietly, his eyes thoughtful. Maybe he's tired. Maybe I'm tired.

"*Want . . .*" I murmur for the last time, and then quite unexpectedly I fall asleep.

Well, really, it was not all that difficult to go on from there. What is a language, after all, but a series of variations on this central theme, a symphony of hopeless desires? In the beginning is the Word, and the Word is *want.* We want food and sex and warmth and death and the rest is only commentary and subterfuge, in my opinion. The rest is only noise.

And so, once I'd achieved the interface of infantile drives and conventional linguistic assignations which Dr. Kai had theorized, in a recent article, would result from PAT, I began to move forward. I had a grip on the essentials, basic information processing; now I was free to explore the middle reaches of the keyboard, the minor notes, the percussives, the tinkling delicacies of phrasing where the music of meaning takes shape. At night I'd lie naked on my little cot, wearing out the batteries in my tape recorder. I filled the darkness with words. It was something like building a fire. Gathering up the tinder of impressions, piling them into thoughts, stoking the thoughts into phrases, kindling the phrases into sentences, the sentences into narratives, until all was warmth and light . . . Oh, I still played with Babe, Kid, and Shorty, of course, but that was more for recreation than instruction. Now my real play was alone, in the privacy of my room. There I fondled language like an instrument I had neglected too long. Ardently I stroked its keys and polished its surfaces until they revealed, shining back, the wonder of my own reflection.

In time I began to grow bored with English and made plans to take up Italian, dabble in German, have a go at Chinese. Was I getting ahead of myself? Perhaps. But then we all were. Dr. Kai put together a new book proposal, and secured a large advance. Three new Vocoders were purchased from Japan. Bloom began to dress in expensive fabrics and affect a European manner. Invitations arrived from conferences in Sydney and Brazil. Amid all this commotion came the news that I was scheduled to be released on the last day of March. My homecoming, then, would be part of the pageantry of renewal that is the suburban spring—the lush grass, the tulips' colorful assertions, the happy little *pock* of tennis balls in the twilight. And us too, Linda and I, side by side on the porch, speaking of all that had gone unsaid between us. I had lost not just language; I had lost time itself. And what was more precious than that?

Finally, the day before I am to return home, Drs. Kai and Bloom invite several researchers from the state university to watch me put through one more call to my brother William. It is a symbolic closure of sorts, a bow on the wrapping of my progress. Almost a lark. As if to underscore how little this means to me, I yawn as I dial the number, feigning boredom.

Then it occurs to me: I *am* bored. Despite if not because of Kai's presence beside me, and three departments' worth of researchers watching from behind the two-way glass, what I feel is, at bottom, a curious detachment from these people and their attentions, and a new, hard-won envelopment in my own affairs. I am almost back in the world, it seems.

Ruth answers again and this time I am prepared for her.

"Ah Ruth! Fair princess of the northwest! Mistress of my only sibling! May my regard for you counterbalance your deficiencies of charm and warmth and all else that plagues you!"

I appear to be a little nervous after all.

"Who the hell *is* this?" demands that good lady.

"I wonder, Ruth, whether you happen to recall William's younger brother?"

There's a brief pause. The phone is crackling a bit, but not terribly. I remain calm. "I'm doing the dishes," Ruth declares, with a conviction I find mysterious.

"Ruth, I note your non sequitur and take comfort in it. Now, may I respectfully ask you to summon William?"

Dr. Kai scribbles furiously on his pad, then shows it to me. *Too formal. Remember the colloquial.*

"Billy!" I hear her calling through the house. "Billy, pick up the phone!"

My brother picks up the extension with a gruff hello. "Hey dude!" I sing out. "How you doing?"

Dr. Kai winces and shakes his head. Too colloquial? *Relax,* he scribbles on the pad.

"Huh?"

"William," I say, "it's your brother."

"Hey," he says, perking up. "How do you like that? The prodigal returns."

Strange, but the sound of William's voice on the line affects me just like the Vocoder. It's such a simple and agreeable set of signals, so much a part of me already, that the words hardly register. Is this a good thing or a bad thing? I appear to have lost track. My self-confidence slips its moorings and begins to drift. Below is a whirling darkness. I can feel its familiar pull.

"Deep breath," Kai whispers. "Remember what's at stake."

"William," I say.

"You know, it's funny, but I was going to call you today. I just had the craziest dream."

"William."

"It was all about you. At least I think it was you. You weren't actually *in* it, but I could hear you yelling from somewhere far away. I don't know, maybe you were underground. Anyway I ran around looking for you, scared out of my wits. The next thing I know Ruth says the phone is ringing, and it's you. She thinks you're pretty wacko by the way."

"William," I say. "I want."

"Huh?"

"I want."

There's a silence for a moment. "I hear you," he says. "I hear you, bro."

"Sex," I say.

He groans. "Tell me about it."

"We're getting older, William. First you, then me."

"You've got that right."

"It's coming, you know. It's on the way."

"I know."

"You know?"

"I know."

And then William begins to speak. It turns out he has a great deal to say on these subjects. He speaks of aches in his body and fears in his mind. He speaks of restless nights and lethargic days, of disappointments in business, in relations with other people, in himself. I can't entirely follow everything that he has to say—there are a great many baffling particulars—but I am aware of what runs below the words, the black current that bears them along. He's alone and afraid. All he says adds up to this. He's alone and afraid, and there's a tremor in his voice, too. For all I know it's been there all along. And now my thoughts turn to Linda and the children, wandering the house these past weeks while I play with my machines. I was right to seek help, but have I sought it from the wrong quarter?

When I hang up I am crying again, not from failure this time but success.

The researchers from the state university press forward with their questions. "Not now," Kai says. He ushers them out and shuts the door.

When we're alone, he looks down at the floor. I can't tell, maybe he's been crying too. "I shall miss you, Mr. Statler."

I have a new word now and I figure it's time to use it. "Love."

He nods and reaches for his glasses.

"Tomorrow," he says, "you will return home."

That night the staff throws me a party down in the PAT room. Everyone is there. Even the toddlers have taken extra-long naps in the afternoon so as to be awake for the festivities. Bloom breaks out several bottles of domestic champagne—for all his airs, he remains a cheapskate—and the tape recorder, which has been appropriated by the younger technicians, has been programmed to play reggae and Motown at the loudest possible volume. I dance for a while but feel awkward and stop. My partner keeps on going. The room is crowded. People wander up to give me hugs, testimonials. Everyone promises to keep in touch. It occurs to me that

I hardly know these people, though I have been around them for several months. And yet they appear to know me. On what basis?

Bloom sits cross-legged on a wrestling mat, flirting with one of the researchers.

I ask him where Kai is. He shrugs.

I decide to look in on the toddlers. They're in the next room over, standing in their cribs, trying to follow the action. Shorty of course is drooling. Babe has a vacant, gassy stare; he appears to be drunk on punch. All three pound their tiny fists in time to the music against the bars of the cribs. For a while I get down on my knees and make some of the old sounds. It feels very odd. I am just wondering what to do next when Dr. Kai comes in.

"You have been asked to make a speech," he informs me. His tie is loose; behind his glasses his lids are droopy and reddened. Can he be drunk?

"Should I?"

He shrugs. "It would be a fitting gesture. A positive manipulation of symbolic behavior. And it might induce them to lower the volume of that deafening noise. I favor the idea."

We emerge together. The lights are turned up; the tape is shut off. Everyone gathers close to listen. I am tired, and have had a good deal to drink, and it takes me some seconds to find a suitable rhythm and tone—I have never been fond of public speaking, even at my best—but in time I have said all the gracious words I can think to say. When I stop the staff applauds boisterously. Many of them appear to be moved. Then the music comes on again, the lights go dim, and people go back to what they were doing, for a while at least, before they reach for their coats and drift away.

• • •

And now here it is the next morning. I am sitting in Kai's office for the last time, staring at the fold of his hands. In twenty minutes Linda will arrive to whisk me down the coast and into my community of old. And I have nothing to say.

"Well," Kai demands, his patience exhausted. "What is it, Mr. Statler?"

I shrug and turn toward the window. It's soaked with light.

"It is too late for this. We have gone too far. I sense from you a new subverbal response. I request that in the interest of our research and, if I may, our friendship, you give it a name."

Hate.

Kindly explain.

Because I miss it. I miss my tremor, my stammer, my whatever you want to call it. I'm not saying it was healthy or productive. But it was mine. Because I was free then and I'm not free now.

How so?

Because to give form to what is formless is to be trapped in lies.

Yes, but to lie is to act, and it is only through action, paradoxically, that we find peace.

"Hey," I say. "That's pretty good."

And then he looks at me strangely, and I realize that the words were not his but mine. Not forms, but approximations of forms. And as such they'll have to serve.

My face grows warm in the gathering light.

So you see how it is, blinks Dr. Kai.

Yes. I see.

There is a freedom, too, in inexactitude. This is true in science as in life. It is perhaps what distinguishes us. Though of course it can be frustrating. Frustrating and messy.

Tell me about it.

He leans forward in his chair. For perhaps the first time in our acquaintance he seems genuinely uncertain what to do with me.

"Be well, Mr. Statler," he says in an officious tone, as if he's pushed a button on his console to switch from one conversation to another which is more pressing. "I wish you all good fortune."

"Goodbye."

It doesn't sound like much, but the message appears to get through intact. We shake hands. Then I leave his office and walk out past the reception area and into the tumult and glare of the morning, rehearsing with each step the first words I will say to my wife.

A Flight of Sparks

Victor Franks, because he worked nights, and perhaps because his metabolism, as his ex-wife once suggested, was slower than average, did not function very well in the morning. He was a man who lacked the few simple habits that breed contentment. Thus when he found himself awake before ten, as he did today, he was not able to walk through the rituals of coffee-making or pet-feeding with his eyes half-closed, the way most of us can, and take a modest comfort in the performance of these small duties. He had loosened his grip on things too far for that. He did not own a reliable coffeemaker any longer—what was the point, when you could buy the stuff on every corner, in every conceivable format? This was pretty much the line of reasoning he applied to food as well. As for pets, his sheepdog Milt, a loving but ungainly specimen, was no longer in his custody, having been struck down by a rogue Pontiac near the marina last year. A traumatic event all around. The driver, bent ashen-faced over the panting dog, had been so aghast at his own carelessness that Victor had forgiven him at once. It was his own carelessness he had not forgiven, his slack hand on the leash, his failure of peripheral vision. Milt, a quick healer, had recovered in less than a month, and was now boarding with Victor's ex-wife. But Victor in his isolation was slower to recuperate. Occasionally he found himself brooding over Milt, more sentimental about the dog than he would have believed possible. At least he told himself it was about the dog.

Because it was still early, he lay for a while in the darkened bedroom, breathing in the jasmine from the side yard and listening to the radios. He kept a little Sony in the kitchen, a giant antique Philco in the living room, and on the bedtable next to his head, a cheap GE with a digital clock, and they were always on. A lot of surface noise was required, it seemed, when you lived alone. And radio was better than television. Less tyrannical. You could shut your eyes with the radio; you could listen and still dream. This morning the news was full of cabals and incursions, shadowy displacements. Borders were being crossed. He should pay attention, Victor thought. One had to stay on top of these things.

Unfortunately he felt very much on the bottom of things at the moment. His head was all gray matter, hazy and indolent; there was only blank space on that easel in his mind meant to hold the sketch of the day's campaign. He'd hardly slept. His eyes were raw, as if bruised by their own sockets. His dreams had lacked color, velocity. It occurred to him, like the punchline to some obscure, half-remembered joke, that he was forty-six years old. Much too old to be this fucked up. Or maybe this was when it was *supposed* to happen, he thought, in the middle years, when the insulation wore thin, and one was forgiven less, and everything counted, every loss, every mistake. Sure, he was right on schedule. He was doing just fine, Victor thought, where loss and mistakes were concerned.

As soon as the phone rang he was able to recall with great clarity why he had set the alarm for nine-thirty. "You're late," said Averick.

He had promised to get to the hospital this morning.

"Not that it matters to me, one way or another. Not that I'm keeping track. Late, early—these are shallow, temporal concerns. They're beneath me."

"Sorry," Victor said. "I was sort of sleeping."

"No hurry," Averick said. "The important thing is you get your rest."

"I'll be there in an hour."

"I may not be here in an hour. I'm feeling really good. I may be out playing golf. Out on the back nine, whaling away with a five-iron. How hard could it be?"

Philip Averick was Victor's lawyer and friend. They'd been roommates in a three-bedroom apartment in Santa Monica, circa 1971. There they endured the draft lottery together, popping the cork on shoplifted Mumm's the night they learned their numbers, drinking to Fate's sloppy but benevolent hand, which had sheltered them so sweetly. But then it always had. They were children of prosperity, of big cars and sweeping lawns; even had their numbers been low their deferments would all but certainly have held. Still, they took nothing for granted. They weren't cynics. The luck of youth had made them extravagant, generous. For a considerable time—longer than the youth, longer than the luck—it had kept them innocent, even good.

The third bedroom had been rented to an unknown comedian named Jerry Slott, who spent twenty or so days every month out on the road, playing Holiday Inns and Ramadas and making the occasional appearance in situation comedies as the skinny big-nosed kid who whined to the star about his problems. As it happened, he was ten years older than he looked, viciously confident, successful with women, and cagey and winsome with men, and Victor and Averick were genuinely sorry when shortly after their graduation from UCLA, Jerry Slott gave up show business to take over his father's shirt factory in New York. Slott too had softened over the years. Out of nostalgia for that golden time before the Garment District, he'd call every few months to recycle the same tinny jokes, the same emptied-out memories of fellowship. Hence two years before, when word began to spread of Averick's diagnosis, the first call he received was Jerry Slott's. Victor, who'd been camping in Utah with Milt, was among the last.

It was a cool clear morning, sunny and without breeze, as Victor left the driveway. His old Fiat seemed at first to be having one of its good days, but when he pulled onto Ashby the transmission began to fight him like the Manichean puppet it was. This air of combat was intensified by the call-in show on the radio, on the very station that employed Victor as a producer. Someone was yelling something at someone, taking part in the daily town meeting of the vulgar, the desperate, the lonely, and the depraved. Victor flipped to KJAS. "Sketches of Spain" embraced him in its wispy arms and then was gone, replaced by the somnolent patter of the jock.

What was needed, Victor thought, was a little less talk and a little more trumpet. But the stations were moving in the other direction, toward the rote shuffling of predictable sounds. A shame. He had not yet lost his love for the processes of radio—for those padded, windowless control rooms, those whisper-perfect mikes—but his interest in the product was gone.

Averick, he imagined, would be listening to the radio too. Also watching TV, talking on the phone, checking his email, and hollering at the nurses. He was a patient at Children's Hospital in

Oakland, which given his behavior was more than apt. If there was any dignity to be won in a stoic decline, Averick did not seem inclined to pursue it. His illness had incensed him to a kind of rabidity. It had come upon him suddenly and when it hit it was with the force of betrayal, a turnaround of the epic project he had conceived for his life. He was a sharp, big-shouldered man, at home in the wide rooms of the powerful; he regarded the tumor inside him as a kind of lame joke, an awkward and embarrassing accident. Its lack of form, its loopy and erratic growth, aroused in Averick something like contempt. If he was going to die from such dumb causes, he was going to do it loudly, with fits of rage and pique; he was going to do it *badly.* Victor thought it an admirable stance, and yet during his sporadic visits he could not entirely suppress a small but palpable distaste. The truth was he felt tyrannized by Averick's candor, and in an oblique way almost envious of him—of his cause, his seriousness of purpose, the air of imminence that hovered over the man's big self-occupied head like the halo of a moon.

When he entered the rectangular room he found Averick propped up by several pillows, dictating a letter into his tape recorder and staring impatiently out the window at the parking lot.

". . . upon receipt of said document, counsel will file the above motion in appellate court . . ." his gaze flickered to the door, noted Victor, then returned to the window, ". . . whereupon a decision should be forthcoming within a period of no less than thirty days' time. In the event that counsel has not medically expired, his retainer will be calculated at that date. Yours sincerely, etc. . . ." He put down the machine and smiled sullenly at Victor. "No rest for the weary, eh?"

"It's nice to see you keeping busy."

"Sure. Busy is easy."

"I'm not so certain about that."

Averick settled in amongst the pillows. "You're not so certain about anything, are you? That's your whole story."

"Maybe so."

"Of course there are worse things you could say about a person. You could say, for instance, a person's got cancer and is going to die. Couldn't you?"

"I suppose you could."

Averick spread his pale arms triumphantly. They had not lost their muscle tone. His hair was still springy and dark, his cheeks still flared with color. His eyes, though, were sunken, and his barrel chest was caving in. "I may not play golf today after all," he said. "I don't have the right shoes."

"Plus you don't know how."

"There's that too. But listen to this. The doc says I'm in remission. He says go home and relax. I'm going to outlive his children is the basic idea."

"That's fantastic, Philip."

"Except guess what. He doesn't have any children. I checked with the nurse; the guy's a fruit. Also a fucking liar. Still, he seems pretty sincere about this remission business. He better be. He knows I'll sue his ass right off if he's wrong."

"So if he says go home, why aren't you home?"

"Don't rush me. I'll be going soon. The thing is, I sort of like it here. People pay attention to me. They look me over carefully. The fellow in the corner bed is a wonderful conversationalist. He knows many things."

Victor glanced over at the corner bed. It was empty. Averick, he assumed, was losing his mind.

"Sit down already." Grunting, he pivoted up on his forearms and shifted position, so he was facing Victor more directly. "You look terrible, Victor. I mean it. You make me look good in comparison."

"Well that's what I'm here for. To cheer you up."

"I didn't say you cheered me up. You don't. Frankly, you're depressing. I'm allowed to say that because of this tumor. It allows me to take liberties, to be honest and unsparing. It's hard not to get malicious. But I'm speaking to you now as your friend of long duration, and I'm telling you frankly that you look really terrible, and my professional advice to you is to shave off that ridiculous beard and go off to some tropical clime and relax. Club Med I hear is a marvelous experience. Go down there and meet a schoolteacher, some very conscientious young woman from Cleveland or Baltimore who works with the handicapped and is impressed by your worldly melancholy, and then fuck her brains out behind the dunes. That's what I'd do if I was you. Of course you'll have to change your clothes. You look like you slept in those mothy pants. You look, if you'll excuse the expression, very divorced."

"Nice day," said Victor, "if it doesn't rain."

"Okay, fine," said Averick. "Now I'll shut up."

"Good."

"You talk. Tell me something. I don't care what. Just talk about yourself and your vision of life and I'll lie here and nod and forget all about my impending death."

"I've been reading about dreams," Victor said. "Their history and so forth."

"Good. Good start. Go on."

"The oldest dream on record is about an empty building. It was told by a woman in Mesopotamia. The overseer of a palace. In her dream she entered the great temple, where the statues of the gods were kept. But the statues were gone. So were all the priests, and the people who worshipped them."

"And then?"

"That was it." Strangely enough, Victor was thinking that he enjoyed these little talks. He always had. Perhaps he enjoyed them too much. "That was the whole dream."

"So what?" asked Averick, querulous. "What are you trying to say?"

"I'm not trying to say anything."

"All this shit about temples. I mean jesus."

"Forget it," Victor said.

"You're not very good at this, are you?"

"I suppose not."

"Do you like me, Vic? I mean, let's be honest with each other. Does the prospect of my dying hurt you? I don't mean the way it hurts me, of course. I just mean, does it hurt. I'm genuinely curious."

"Yes," Victor said. "Yes, it hurts."

"And you'd like to be a good friend, wouldn't you? Under the circumstances I mean. You'd like to make me better, or at least make me *feel* better, or at least make *yourself* feel better, though not in a way that would actually make *me* feel worse. Isn't that right?"

"Isn't what right?"

Averick grinned wearily. "Touché."

"I'm not trying to be clever."

"I know you're not. I'm just having some fun with you. Listen, what I'm trying to get at here is something specific. A favor."

"Go ahead."

"It requires some prefacing first. Because it's not a little favor. It's not a will-you-lend-me-some-money or can-I-borrow-your-lawn-mower favor. It's a large, significant favor, the kind one should probably never ask of anyone, unless of course one happens to have a tumor the size of a grapefruit affixed to one's aorta and windpipe, and one happens to be talking to one's oldest friend in the world, cold and forbidding place that it is."

Victor reached over to pluck a tulip from the bouquet on the nightstand that Averick's firm had sent over the week before. It sagged dryly as he twirled the stem. "Are we done with the preface?"

"I want you to take a vacation."

Victor laughed.

"No, not that Club Med stuff, that wasn't serious. I have something else in mind. A week's vacation, all expenses to be paid by the party of the second part, i.e., me. I want you to get on a plane and fly down to Mexico, land of contrasts."

"What's in Mexico?"

"History, Victor. History everywhere. The Mayans, the Aztecs. Chichén Itzá. Ancient Palenque. Awesome shrines. Timeless cities. The ruins of the past. Also," he said, suppressing a small cough, "my daughter."

Averick had never been married, to Victor's knowledge, though for much of the 1980's he had lived with a woman named Celia Lockhart, a sweet, recessive neurotic who ran a flower store near the Berkeley campus. Apparently the shop had expanded, and grown into something of an empire. Now Celia was coming into her own. She and Averick were still friends; she stopped by to visit regularly at the hospital, on her way to pick up her girls at their private school.

"No, not with Celia."

"With who then?"

"Your skeptical look is duly noted," Averick said. "But that's because you don't remember Donna Gans."

"Sure I do. She was that skinny painter with the Volkswagen

who lived off Melrose. She wore black sleeveless teeshirts and a lot of earrings. She liked to humiliate you in restaurants. Who could forget Donna Gans?"

"Evidently neither of us."

"Also you talk about her all the time."

Averick nodded sadly. "She was the one, Victor. We all have one and Donna was mine. Unfortunately, I wasn't hers. The oldest story in the world."

"And this daughter in Mexico?"

"Here's the thing. Six weeks after we broke up Donna went down to Baja, shacked up with that surfer, Jorge I think his name was. They had a kid, a girl, p.d.q. She told me so herself. This was nineteen years ago, more or less."

"And so?"

"Victor, the kid, she could be mine. I don't know, it's just a feeling. But I think she's mine. And I want to see her, just once. See what she's made of. It would help to know I had a kid out there somewhere. Someone, you know, of substance. It's the kind of moving little personal melodrama one should go out on."

"According to the doctor, one may not be going out."

"Sure." Averick nodded as though deep in thought, but Victor could see he wasn't listening. "It would be a service, Vic. It would be, as our people say, a *mitzvah.* What do you say?"

After a moment, Victor said, "No."

There must have been something wrong with the inflection of his voice, however, because Averick was nodding contentedly, his gaunt face lit like a buoy.

"No," he repeated. "And stop grinning at me. I've got troubles of my own. The last thing I need is to perform your morbid errands."

At that moment the nurse came in, wheeling a big red-faced Irishman toward the corner bed. Victor could see the man's spine, pale and erratic, through the narrow space where his smock tied up in back. "Hello Mr. Murphy," boomed Averick. "How're the kids today?"

"Hush," said the nurse. "Mr. Murphy is very tired." She settled Murphy onto the bed, checked his chart, adjusted the drapes slightly, and then came over to direct at Averick a look of officious petulance. "And how are we feeling this morning?"

"Like we're on a great adventure, Nurse Patty." Averick grinned and fluttered his lids. "Like we're out in the jungle, hunting for big game. Ask my friend here." He coughed, indicating Victor with a wave of his hand. "Tell her, Vic. Tell her who she's dealing with."

Victor got to his feet. He had to fight the impulse to put his hands in his pockets. "You have to forgive him," he said to the nurse. "He thinks he's the star of the movie."

"I like movies," she said, and smiled blankly as he left the room.

It was obviously some illness of his own, thought Victor, watching the continent swallow the winged shadow of the plane. There was no other explanation. Among the bonds that tied him to Philip Averick, a quest such as this had no precedent; it was a transmutation of loyalty into recklessness, sense into nonsense. He brooded over it as the plane hurtled southeast. At last he found, at the bottom of his third glass of scotch, an idea that he liked: Averick was actually doing *him* a favor. He'd been sent to Mexico not on some ludicrous whim, but as a deliberate act of mercy, the opportunity to escape his friend's decline without dishonor. Averick had done the selfless, farsighted thing, and set him free.

Or had he?

Donna Gans, at last report—the news was several years old—had moved to the Yucatán, where she managed a small two-star tourist hotel in Mérida. Whether or not she was still with Jorge they'd been unable to ascertain; Averick's sources when it came to Donna had never been particularly reliable. Still, he liked to work the phones. The absence, not the presence, was what engaged a man's energies. The prospect of connection with the unseen. It was the same thing that had brought him to radio, Victor thought. He stood in the terminal, fingering the slip of paper containing the hotel's address, and waiting for his luggage to arrive on the enormous belt.

Though it was January, the air was steamy and flooded with sunlight. He had to squint to see the horizon. Thick low-slung jungle, only ten feet high, was invading the airport area, buckling the tarmac and threatening the roads. Palm trees with yellow flowers bowed toward his taxi as he sped into town. The streets were narrow, with tiny sidewalks. All the buildings were low to the ground, except for the massive cathedral that loomed over the *zocalo,* dwarfing the flowers in shadow. Victor could smell their blossoms from the car. There was a transistor radio on the dashboard, tinkling a pop tune. The back of the driver's head swayed benignly to the melody.

"Hotel del Prado, *señor.*"

The fare, as he understood it, came to several thousand pesos. He fumbled in his pocket for the unfamiliar bills, reminding himself that the exchange rate made this a very small sum indeed. Regardless, Averick was footing the bill. He was being carried. He would have to get used to it.

Though the façade of the hotel was all but indistinguishable from the colorless plaster of the neighboring apartment houses, inside he found another world, a lush courtyard of bougainvillea and guano palms, their limbs ascending toward the balconies, their leaves drooping moistly over the iron railings. The air was cool. A tiny lizard stood frozen on the bottom stair, arrested between the solid geometry of the tiles and the profuse disorder of the garden. Victor imagined a whole city of hidden life inside the walls, under the floor, staking out the interstices of the cultivated and the wild.

"Señor?"

He could hardly believe his luck. The girl at the reception desk was about the right age, light-skinned, precociously solemn, her features a compromise of racial alignments; she did not look entirely Mayan, though she wore what seemed the standard folk dress, a white smock adorned with red and blue flowers. When she spoke to him she averted her eyes, but not before he saw, latent in her dark stare, some of Averick's irony and loathing. *"Habla Ingles?"* he asked, trying to conceal his eagerness.

She nodded yes, but vaguely.

"Is your mother here? I'd like to talk to your mother."

The girl inclined her head in his direction, as though he had only just embarked upon what was to be a long, entertaining narrative. Behind the desk, one bare foot came up to scratch at the back of her calf.

"Your mother," Victor repeated, his face crowding with blood. "*Donde? Donde* your mother?"

"Mama?" she asked. "Mama?"

He thought perhaps she was an idiot, or else he was, or else they both were. But then from a darkened room under the stairs a thin, tired voice answered hers. The girl said something in Spanish, and looked at Victor expectantly, as if waiting for him to prove himself an object worthy of study. Finally the mother came out. Of course she wasn't Donna Gans, anyone could see that. She was an Indian, under five feet tall, a woman who could not have been nearly so old nor so exhausted as she looked just now in the fading dusk, shuffling toward him in her blue robe and slippers. Though he had awakened her from her nap she smiled tolerantly at Victor and reached for the hotel registry with no special urgency. *"Buenos días,"* she said wanly. "You would like a room?"

He nodded.

"You have your wife with you?"

"No. I'm here on business, you see."

"Business." She reached for a key in the recesses of her desk. She knew about business. They discussed the price; considering the opulence of the lobby he thought it absurdly cheap. As for the room, it was plain and clean. There was no air conditioner, but she showed him the switch for the ceiling fan and pointed out the bottles of mineral water on the bureau. She had only been managing the hotel for six months, she told him; before that, she had run a rental car agency in Cancún. She did not know a *Señora* Gans.

When he'd showered and changed clothes he went into town and found a small restaurant just off the *zocalo.* Only a handful of other tourists were out that early. He drank several beers with dinner, stretching out the evening's anonymity as long as he could. Hammock vendors strolled past with their showy nets. One boy came over to his table and dangled his hammock hopefully, pointing out the quality of the weave, but Victor shook his head and the boy scooted off after more promising game. He should have bought a hammock, Victor thought. It would make a nice gift for someone. He remained in the restaurant until half past ten, by which time it was abundantly clear to him that he was drunk. The fact did not surprise him, but it was somewhat alarming; it went against what he'd thought were his intentions. He had come down here hoping to regain some of his control, but he saw it would not be that easy a matter.

In his book he read of the city's motto, bestowed by King Philip of Spain: *Very Noble and Very Loyal.* King Philip indeed.

On the way back to the hotel he found a phone booth that wasn't occupied and he stopped to call Averick at the hospital. A block away, on the steps of the Palacio, some sort of rally was in progress. An older man stood at the microphone, pompously reciting what sounded to Victor's ears like very bad poetry. Someone strummed a guitar. Leaning into the shell of the phone booth, he waited until the night administrator had established beyond a reasonable doubt that Philip Averick was no longer listed as a patient, then he hung up. The speaker was still at the microphone, declaiming for all he was worth.

He'd call Averick at home the next morning, he decided.

Back in his room he gave himself over to fatigue, and lay down on the soft cot breathing mulch from the garden below. He did not so much sleep as drift on slow tides toward morning.

The next day he put his call through again and had no better luck at Averick's house. He was on his own. The thought fixed him with irritation for a minute. Then, abruptly, he became exhilarated. He was on his own, free to pursue his own ends.

He bought some new sunglasses in a kiosk and walked through the marketplace. On the crowded sidewalk he felt tall and airy, newly evolved, a creature of his own imagining. He strolled from stall to stall, following the shoppers. There was no need to hurry. The bounty of a continent was laid out before him. But as he ventured deeper into the maze of stalls the air grew close, uncomfortably warm. Much of the fruit was rotting. Flies swarmed over the denuded pork. His enthusiasm for shopping began to dissipate. He looked at everything but bought nothing. A long finger of sweat trickled down his ribs. It occurred to him that there was not a soul on the planet who knew where he was at this moment. He himself wasn't sure. At some point in his travels he had become thoroughly, hopelessly lost.

Good, he thought. Now it begins.

When he emerged at last from the thicket of vendors, he drifted into the nearest travel agency, where he booked a car for later that afternoon.

Back at the Hotel del Prado the woman who had shown him his room was sweeping dead canna petals into a pile. She was in the same robe and slippers as the night before, and apparently the same spirits. Her gaze took in Victor dispassionately as he nodded at her over his new sunglasses. It was not until his foot reached the third stair that he heard her say, "*Señor.*"

He turned and leaned over the railing.

"*Señora* Gans. I find out she is not here."

"Yes, thank you," said Victor.

"She has gone to the coast, *señor.* Long time. They think maybe she is on Cozumel. No sure."

He looked at her regretfully. She had done him a service, gone out of her way, and though he should have been grateful, he felt somehow constrained by the information; it exerted a regressive pull. "Thank you," he said again, and went on up the stairs to pack.

For three days he drove in the jungle, touring the ruins by day and passing his evenings in the bars of the archaeological motels. He'd sit alone at a table by the window—careful, as so many tourists are, to separate himself from other tourists—and read books he picked up along the way. The books were histories of the Mayans and the Mexicans, full of conquests and escapes, of rebirth through adventure and the rules of conduct by which great peoples lived, and reading them was like scratching a deep, obscure itch he had not known was there. Outside the jungle hummed and ticked with nocturnal energies. It was a very low-slung and unthreatening jungle, as jungles go. Still, he supposed it was possible to get lost in it. Even here, in this stunted, poor man's wilderness, you could wander off the path and not come back. *Don't sleep too much,* he read, *or you'll become a dreamer . . .* Was that what he was doing? Losing himself? Embracing the ruins as his own? He was finding it more and more difficult to remember.

The fourth morning he made for the coast.

In Tulum he hiked down to the ruins and looked them over halfheartedly—they were halfhearted ruins to begin with—until the crowd grew oppressive, whereupon he headed over to the beach and kicked off his sandals. The sand was remarkably clean and cool, as smooth as the sea itself. The water was a patchwork of greens and blues, shallows and sudden depths. He waded in a few steps. Half a dozen snorkels could be seen circling out in the channel. He made up his mind to go snorkeling the next day. In three days his week would be up, and what would he have to show for it? He had bought no souvenirs, sent no letters or postcards. He had not marked his journey any more than his feet had marked this sand. Tomorrow he would drive up the coast to Playa del Carmen and rent some equipment. If he wanted to, he could always catch the ferry to Cozumel from there.

He noticed then a young man or old boy—about eighteen, he thought—with almost impossibly blond hair, regarding him from a distance of some ten yards downwind. A snorkel and fins were piled neatly at his feet. "You okay, man?"

Victor realized that he'd been muttering to himself. "I was just . . ." he offered a shrug to express inner complexity, "just working things out."

"Hey, that's cool." The boy, encouraged, moved cautiously forward. "That's what it's for, right?"

He spoke in the dreamy, untroubled tones endemic to southern California. He was tall and thin, pink-nosed, wearing a bathing suit patterned with sea horses. Victor was pretty sure he was stoned. Beneath his placid smile there was the suggestion of something belligerent, a dogmatic insistence on naming exactly what things were for. "You got to envy those fishies. Just flop around in all that blue wonder all day. Fish, they've got the right idea. They know how it's done all right. They got the big fella's ear."

Victor nodded, waiting for the boy to get bored and go away.

"I mean, check out the action on those reefs. The colors. Down there you know, you know?"

"You know you know what?"

"It's not just us. There's something else. The fishies, they know all about it. They're wise. They've got *knowledge.*" He came in closer. "Bum a cigarette? I'm all out."

"Sorry. *No mas.*"

"Don't worry about it. Shit kills your wind anyway. You here for the ruins or the water?"

"I was just thinking of doing some snorkeling."

"Best place is up at Xel-Ha. Best snorkeling in the galaxy, man."

"I was headed up that way."

"Whereabouts?"

"Maybe Playa del Carmen. I may go to Cozumel from there."

"Ugh. Forget it. Place's totally gone to the dark side. But Playa's still cool. They got this good cake shop right off the beach. Water's clean. Good place to chill."

"It sounds like just the thing."

"Snorkeling's better at Xel-Ha, though."

"Well, I have some business to deal with, too."

The boy narrowed his eyes. "You a developer?"

"Do I look like a developer?"

"Shit, man. What do I know? My dad looks a normal person, and he's some fucking investment manager."

"I'm just looking for a friend. That's all. I came here to find someone."

"Whoa," the boy said, backing away. "I don't want to know, alright? I'm a loyal American, hey. Registered to vote and everything."

Victor laughed. He himself hadn't voted in years.

"Look, I don't want to be rude, but I got a bus to catch." He extended his right hand with curious formality in Victor's direction. Victor took it, gazing with unexpected tenderness into the boy's reddened, vacant eyes. All the children were down here, it seemed. Everyone's daughters and everyone's sons.

"Maybe I'll catch you in Playa later," the boy said. Then he gathered up his snorkel and fins, and hurried down the beach to the bus.

He found Donna Gans pretty much by accident the next morning. He'd spent the night in Playa and risen early, intending to rent some snorkel gear and head out to the reefs north of town. The scuba shop, however, did not adhere to its posted hours, so to kill some time Victor had gone for a walk along the beach. The sand was not nearly so pleasant as Tulum's; it gave off a distinct odor of sewage as he approached the newer bungalows. Still, it was nice to be out there in the early morning. He worked his way north until the buildings thinned out, and there was only one last series of thatched huts between himself and the surrounding jungle. And there, tangled in an elaborate rainbow hammock, holding a paperback volume of Jane Austen over her face like a compact mirror—there was Donna Gans.

She wore a modest one-piece bathing suit and a jade pendant around her neck. Her skin was dark, stretched by sun. She was thinner than Victor remembered, flatter in the chest, longer and more angular in every direction, so much so that it seemed possible, even likely, that she was someone else. But she wasn't. He knew she wasn't, knew it with a cold, intuitive clarity that he found both remarkable and sad. The sight of her was like a taste of the world's smallness, its delicate balance of the unknown and the known, which was forever threatening to tip one way or the other, and as he approached her he had ample time to reflect on this, and to study her without her noticing, for her head was inclined against her inland shoulder. He was all but standing on top of her when she finally lowered her book and turned to see him. "Hi," she said, with no special feeling. "How's the water this morning?"

"Looks fine," he said. "I haven't been in."

"Oh." She lifted her book again.

"You don't remember me," Victor said. The faint air of lament in his voice irritated him. "I knew you a long time ago. In L.A."

Her head swung back. She raised one hand to shade her eyes, and looked him over unhurriedly.

"My name's Victor Franks. I was a friend of Phil Averick's. We roomed together on Fourth Street."

Her mouth went slack. "Mother of god," she moaned. "You're that awful comedian."

"That was someone else," he said. "I was the one who did radio shows. Victor."

"Victor Franks." She squinted through her raised hand.

"That's right."

He watched her face soften and yield as she tried to fit the name onto a recognition. He was glad she didn't bother to pretend, that she had the patience to summon memory and wait. Then, once it arrived, she smiled slowly, grandly, as though in triumph. "Victor," she said. "Victor."

"That's right."

"Hey, how are you, Victor? Good lord. What brings you down this way?"

"Actually," he said, "it's a long story."

"I bet." She fidgeted in the hammock. "I'd ask you to sit down, but as you can see . . ."

"How about if we grab a cup of coffee? It would be nice to talk."

"I don't drink coffee," she said brightly. "But you can buy me some mango juice. Here, give me a hand. I'm getting too old for this thing."

He helped her climb out of the hammock, and together they ducked under the palms and went up a flight of stairs, to a small patio restaurant called the Blue Heron. It was a spare, clean dining room with simple wood tables and an unobstructed view of the sea. Chet Baker was crooning on the stereo, romancing no one at all. They were the only customers in the place.

"You like it?" Donna asked when they were seated. "You better like it. I own the place. Say something nice."

"I like it."

"Praise the lord." She grinned and brought her hands together. "He likes it. Actually, we're doing very well, thank you. The whole town's on the move, but this—this is the nicest spot. Best view, and I've got the only decent cook in the area. I'm a regular success story."

"I'm happy for you," Victor said, though he did not know her well enough to mean it in any but the most general sense. He wondered for an instant if she attracted him, or vice versa. He should know these things by now. He was almost tempted, listening to her talk, to confess his confusion about what was happening to him up north, about the massive blurring at this juncture of his life where he had expected shape and definition. Perhaps this—she—was his fate, and that was why Averick had sent him here. But that made no sense. She was someone else's femme fatale, perhaps several people's; he was no longer so arrogant as to believe that the world's currents of energy flowed in a single direction. Averick was, but maybe Averick had to be. It was the sort of conceit that gave him adrenaline, that helped marshal his force.

As if on cue, Donna Gans set down her juice and sighed. "Okay, I'm ready."

"Ready for what?"

"Tell me about Phil. How is the boy? Still defending hoodlums in the barrio?"

"It's been a long time, hasn't it?"

"Oh," she said. "That means he's somewhere else, doesn't it."

"Yes."

"Wait, don't tell me. He works on Wall Street and commutes to Connecticut. He votes for moderate Republicans. His kids attend the best schools. At night he makes calls for the UJA. Why don't you stop me already? This is getting me down."

"He's none of those things," said Victor.

"I know. I was just playing."

"He works for a small firm in Oakland. Mostly labor stuff, nonprofit. He isn't married. As for politics, he still reads *The Nation.*"

"So what, then? He's got cancer or something?"

"Yes."

She smiled privately, as if he had said something very different.

"It began in his jaw and then it went away and then it came back a few months ago in his lungs. It's hard to sort out exactly where it's going next. Before I left it was under control, whatever that means."

She listened, asking no questions, as he told her everything else he knew of Averick's condition. Then they sat there in silence for a minute or two. Victor looked out through the palm fronds at a lone pelican, skimming the brilliant water in search of prey. It glided without effort, a slim white bow across the great blue stringed instrument that was the sea. He's after those wise fish, Victor thought.

"Well shit," Donna said finally. "You're not exactly making my day here."

"I know."

"It's so pretty, isn't it. Look. You can see all the way to Cozumel."

"It's beautiful."

"And the people, they're wonderful. The Indians I mean. You know what I like about them? They know about some things and not others. They know about food and drink and song and God. These things they know. They're weak on data, no question. They don't analyze or process well when it comes to data. There's a lot of corruption in the local government. Distribution of services is deeply flawed. The whole country's a mess, in fact, and the poverty is horrifying, and it's boring and slow around here, and half my customers are old Germans who did christ knows what in the war, and I miss going out to concerts with my friends, who I hardly get to see anymore unless somebody dies or else comes down here, which for all I know is the same thing. What I'm trying to say is there are any number of reasons why it's a really bad life choice to stay down here. But I can't leave."

"You don't have to explain yourself," Victor said. "Not to me."

She cocked her head and squinted at him, as she had on the beach. "I don't?"

"No."

"Then why are you here? What does Averick want?"

He considered the question. "A legacy, I think."

"Come again?"

"Or maybe a redemption."

"You're going to have to work a little harder at clarity, Victor."

"He mentioned something about a daughter," Victor said. "He thought she might be his. He wanted me to find out for him."

"A daughter?"

Donna Gans leaned back in her wicker chair. After a moment, her face contorted into laughter. Her shoulders twitched spasmodically; her black hair, flecked with gray, tumbled across her cheeks. Victor waited for her to stop. He didn't really mind. It was pleasant just sitting there, carrying through with his errand; he didn't care so much what happened at the end of it.

"I'm sorry," she said, wiping at her eyes. "It's just so unexpected. I miss him so much all of a sudden." She shook her head violently, as if to clear it. "Hoo boy. This is really pitiful."

"I take it he's mistaken," said Victor.

"The poor cluck. What a number we all pull on each other. How dumb and fantastic."

She retreated again into her private thoughts. Her face had changed; she looked quite beautiful all of a sudden, her tanned cheeks aglow with either pride or sorrow, maybe both. To be thought of in such a way, so many years after the fact, to learn that all this time you remained in place, sealed in the amber of memory—no wonder she glowed. She looked like she'd been given back something she'd forgotten having lost, a tiny golden ring from some irreplaceable vault.

The young girl who had served them their juice and coffee came forward now to whisper something in Donna's ear. They exchanged a few sentences in Spanish, then the girl moved off in the direction of the kitchen. Donna turned to Victor and gave him a wry, pensive smile. "No," she said. "That isn't her."

"It's none of my business. But a guy can't help being curious."

"Of course you can't. It's just that it's so ridiculous I'm ashamed to talk about it." She examined her nails, frowning at the irregularities. "The fact is I don't have a daughter. I never did. Understand?"

"Not really, no."

"I don't have a daughter. Or a son either. Children don't work for me, I'm afraid. I've never even had an abortion. The point is," she said, "it was just something I told Philip at the time, to get him off my back."

Two flies lit on the table between them and performed a skittish dance.

"I thought, knowing him, he wouldn't give up otherwise. I didn't want him to wait around for me, put his life on hold. I didn't want him to wait, okay? I know it wasn't honest or fair. But I was trying, christ, Victor, I was trying to be *kind."*

She began to laugh again, quietly and without mirth. One elbow, jerking around to cradle her head, knocked over her glass of juice. The juice spread in a rich yellow pool, thinning as it ran, seeking out the cracks and imperfections in the surface of the wooden table. It was hot out now; the flies were gathering around their heads. Victor stood up, took off his teeshirt, and dabbed at the pool of juice. When he had done all he could he backed away, announcing in a loud voice, "I'm going to go snorkeling now."

He had left his shirt behind at the restaurant, he had not excused himself to Donna, he had not called Averick, he had gone off without having eaten when in fact he was very hungry, and without any clear direction as to which were the proper reefs to explore—and yet Victor felt oddly hopeful once he hit the beach, awash in light. The sun was directly overhead; his body cast no shadow. He took long, smooth strides across the sand. At the scuba shop, he rented a snorkel and mask and some fins that made the simple act of walking an altogether more thoughtful and ambitious activity, and when he was ready he lowered himself into the green shallows, and pushed off from the bottom with his feet. He felt clean and strong. His mouth fit the acrid plastic of the snorkel like a pacifier. It didn't bother him that other people's mouths had fit over it too. He was glad for the company, in a way. He could hear the subtle rhythm of his breath in his ears as he glided through the water. The sea was cool, cool and textured and riddled with light, and there were particles that were floating and others that were sinking, and still others that were swimming along happily toward the stands of coral that flared up from the reefs like a flight of sparks, and for a while he was certain he could stay down there forever. It was like being on the radio, he thought. Just space and waves, active and passive signals; it enveloped you and protected you in one continuous flow of energy, and you could lie down inside it and let it carry you away and from the clamor of the land be exempt. Only something funny was happening. Something wrong. The colors were dimming as he moved ahead. Pretty soon he couldn't really see all that well, and then, not too long after that, he found it hard to maintain his depth. No one could, he was sure of it, this could not have been unique to him, he could not have lost so much of his competence. He fought to see, and to stay down among the silent, indifferent fish, but he had to come up, he had to, because the mask had clouded over with the residue of his own breath.

The Boys at Night

The baby arrived in summer. That was how we referred to her, *the baby.* No name, no gender, just the thing that she was, as if infancy was not a passing condition but a defining one. In her case, it was. But then we were all in need of some defining that summer. I was fourteen though I acted younger, Paulie was eleven but seemed much older, and my parents, those large, irritable people who sat across from us at dinner, were hovering warily around forty, and all the tedious complications that seemed to involve.

Complications. That was what they called it when my mother, during the last trimester of the pregnancy, was ordered by the doctor to relax in bed. It was like a punishment for not being young anymore, for being so brazen as to expect to have a baby after all these years. My mother of course was famously high-strung; it was a cruelty to expect her to relax in bed or anywhere else. Nervous-fingered, impulsive, kinky hair springing like Medusa's from her head, even in sleep she was never quite still but lay coiled on her side shuddering involuntarily, like some tall, toppled animal assaulted by dreams.

For the baby's sake, however, she tried. She spent seven weeks in the bedroom, reading magazines and eating yogurt in front of the fan. The yogurt made her fat and the idleness made her miserable. From the windows came the mockery of the big cars outside, rumbling toward the parkway. Grackles dive-bombed in the mulberry trees. The lawn mowers were roaring, the neighbors' kids splashing in their above-ground pools. You could hear it all from her window. We knew, because as soon as school had ended we'd stopped going out too, and took turns keeping her company. It was like we were all under the same edict: relax, hang out, stay close.

My father, who was better suited to indolence than the rest of us, had to pick up the slack around the house. So he was miserable too. The four of us had become competitors in that arena. After dinner my mother would waddle off back to bed with a novel and a box of cookies, and the rest of us would groan, push back our chairs, and start clearing the table, grumbling about how much we hated doing the dishes, even though it wasn't particularly hard and didn't take particularly long. In fact I *liked* doing the dishes. It was pleasant, sticking my hands in those warm, lazy suds, losing myself in something so mindless and easy, so achievable. And I needed to lose myself. I was restless and unfocused and I looked like a piece of shit. My hormones had declared free agency. Every few hours my forehead would hemorrhage a new pustule, some new patch of fuzz would erupt on my chin, and the timbre of my voice would zoom off on another bobsled run around the room. At school my grades had gone into free fall the year before, but now my popularity, that tenuous safety net I'd stitched together so carefully over the years, was coming unwoven. Girls, with their fine radar, veered away. Teachers lost their geniality. Even my guidance counselor, who was as jaded as they came, professed to be shocked by my descent. I'd better shape up, she informed me, with a wave of my thickening file; I was in danger of "slipping between the cracks."

You can't slip *between* cracks, I wanted to say, you can only slip *through* them. But I wasn't sure I could tell the difference anymore. In any case it didn't matter. I was slipping; things were cracking. And the summer was making it all worse. My friends were busy or away and my family had for all intents and purposes taken up residence on Saturn. Occasionally after the table was wiped clean and the dishes were put away, my father and Paulie and I would go out and walk in the park behind the elementary school—walks whose sole purpose, so far as I could tell, was to allow my father room and time to smoke—and I'd think, yeah, okay, good, let's *go.* But where? In the twilight my father looked distant and tired, unprepared for the rigors of a journey. Deep lines squirmed around on his brow. Here he was, he seemed to be thinking, out with his two golden sons: what now? Or was he thinking about us at all? He used to live in the city, maybe he was thinking about that, old times on Rivington Street when he was still trying to be a painter, hanging out in galleries with some of the people whose pictures he'd show us when they turned up in the *Times* (afterwards, he'd close the paper quietly and head off to smoke) . . . he used to run around a lot I guess, wear black clothes, go to parties with interesting people, but now he was out here teaching at the prep school and shopping for deals on paper towels at the Grand Union like everyone else. That was the story, so far as I understood. He used to be on the move, but then he too had slipped through a crack, acquired some clumsy new weight that made running around impractical and distant, immature. Possibly we were that weight, Paulie and I. Possibly we should have helped him out, lost ourselves more than we did, left him alone. But we just didn't feel like it. The heat was making us sullen and balky; in our ears the insects whined like kazoos. Besides, why give him special treatment? All of us were edgy that summer, not just him.

Toward my mother I was inclined to be more sympathetic.

There was no guesswork with my mother, no concealment. She had a transparency in her face that allowed you to see through the skin, down to the capillaries in their bright expressive clusters. She was a lawyer—when she worked, she worked; when she didn't, she didn't. It was that simple. On weekends she slept late, spent money, saw matinees. My father rarely joined her in these activities—he'd be grading papers or working on the lawn—but I did. Call it what you want, I was her date. I was the one sitting next to her at every bad movie that came to town. I was the one beside her licking popcorn butter off my fingers while she laughed at the dialogue or gaped at some apocalyptic explosion. I was the one who'd linger in the dark as the credits came up, feeling almost implicated in her reluctance to get up and return to the pallid afternoon.

Mama's boy, my father called me once, when I'd taken her side in a meaningless argument. He knew it, I knew it. It would not have surprised me if in the giddy whirl of her thoughts my mother had had occasion to use the phrase herself. As for Paulie, he must have seen it too, even if he didn't want to see it, didn't want to believe, as what kid does, that he had no chance at that title himself. He never said a word, not even that disastrous night at the bowling alley when he probably should have. But then none of us were ourselves that night. No one but the baby. And that was the problem.

I should not blame too much on the baby. As I said, things were already going very badly before she arrived.

Take football.

My body, not content with the havoc it was causing to my face, had recently and on its own authority taken on two and a half inches and nine extra pounds of bulk—at the same time jettisoning my brain, it appeared, altogether—thus emboldening me to go out for football. At the time, early August, it seemed like the thing to do. Football players were at the top of the power chart. They knew what they were doing every afternoon, and with whom, and toward what end. There were clear goals and straight lines and the fellowship of other mean, freakishly oversized people. And there were no cuts; anyone who wanted to be on the junior varsity was given a uniform and put on the roster, if they stuck it out. Which I surely would have done, in my opinion, had I not managed to break my wrist instead.

We were doing tackle drills at the time. Tackling, we were given to understand, was a fundamental aspect of the football experience, and so the coaches could hardly be blamed for insisting that we practice them over and over, like piano scales, say, in order to ensure a good performance. Tackles were meant to be crisp and sure, executed in a certain way. There was a sound you listened for, a brief thud of impact, followed by the crumple and hiss of a body folding in on itself. The sound of good execution.

I was not a very gifted football player, a fact that was becoming increasingly clear to me in the first few weeks of practice, though it was not yet solidly established, I don't think, in the minds of everyone else. To compensate I tried to get by being smart. I listened closely, learned to anticipate the direction of the play so my lack of foot speed and generally sub-par hand-eye coordination wouldn't show. Late in the third week, toward the end of a long hot afternoon session, I caught a break. One of the guards forgot to pull on a sweep, and I had a clear shot at Roger Kelly, the starting halfback, making his turn upfield. I zeroed in. Throwing myself forward, I aimed low at his knees with my helmet. Sure enough, he went down in a heap. I could hear his breath hissing away like a punctured tire. It was extremely gratifying.

The coaches, blowing their whistles, called everyone over to watch me execute the tackle again. Roger dusted himself off and, coolly, without a glance in my direction, took another handoff. This time he slanted outside tackle. I went right after him, crossing my legs like a crab, no longer quite so worried that they would get all tangled up but thinking instead that maybe I had a future in this game after all. About five yards downfield, our paths crossed. Roger saw me coming and lowered his head. I could see in his eyes that he was growing a little tired of this particular drill.

I did not hit him quite so low or so crisply as before, but I got enough of him—or maybe it was the other way around—that this time we both went down. At the bottom of the pile, as it turned out, lay my left arm. Only it no longer much resembled my left arm, or anyone else's; it was dangling at a peculiar, listless angle, like a broken branch. And that was that. Compound fracture. Three months in a cast. Roger, shaken up, sat out a few plays, drank some Gatorade, and went on to a fine season.

Well, said my father on the drive home, a little adversity might not be a bad thing. Test of character, you know.

No one likes having their character tested, in my experience, and why should they? Very few of us ever pass. Though I was to learn a great deal about my threshold for adversity in the weeks that followed, most of what I remember was how boring and enervating a thing adversity really was, and how great was my desire to live a life free of it, and how terrified I was that now that we'd become acquainted, adversity and I were fated to be friends for life.

Stuck at home all day, there were no checks whatever on my sense of boredom and superfluity. My friends were either on vacation or on the team or otherwise engaged, and Paulie—we were, after all, close in our way—was busy with the Summer Science

Fair and the assortment of weird, intricate indoor projects that had occupied his attention for as long as I could remember. Never before had I been particularly curious about how my brother spent his free time. But now, as I performed my sullen rounds through the too-quiet house, I'd find myself loitering at his bedroom door, watching him conduct his chemistry experiments, or tinker with a homemade radio, or take notes for one of his screenplays about the Middle Ages. These were the activities that kept him so wonderfully insulated from the common weather. At times I almost envied him this cerebral bubble of his, this dorky oblivion. Once I looked in and found him running through some old Marx Brothers routines with Harold and Steve, his only friends. They weren't bad either. I figured they'd invite me to join them but somehow they didn't. So much for fraternity.

All of which is only to say that from my point of view, it was almost a relief when the baby showed up.

My mother went into the hospital on a Friday morning and did not come out until Tuesday night. Aunt Millie drove up from Baltimore to stay with us. Millie was a big, high-hipped redhead with a grudge against half the world—the male half. Her mistreatment at the hands of this demographic group had, I gathered, come very early and then matured over the years, so that by this point it was already something of a trademark complaint, like the cost of henna, the barbarism of the Arabs, and the stinginess of the JCPenney corporation, where she was employed as a buyer. Neither of us liked her much. She had a habit of talking very quickly, often to herself, and she tried too hard to be jolly. Also she drank a great deal of water. Whether she was on medication, or these were merely neurotic by-products of loneliness, I don't know. Genetics, that merciless lottery, had awarded my mother the good looks and the romantic disposition; poor Millie, the younger sister, had been left the grudges, the shrewd temper, and the child-bearing hips, but no child. Still, we weren't blind to the heroism of our aunt's cheerfulness. The sight of her basting a chicken for our dinner, her apron (brought up from Baltimore) tied neatly at the back of her neck, her plucked eyebrows knitted in sober concentration—it would have been a little heartbreaking, had we cared more about Millie than we did. But she meant little to us. She was just a sub, with a sub's tone deafness, a sub's ineffectuality and irrelevance. She'd turn out prodigious meals that nobody liked and sit there with me and Paulie, clacking her nails on the table as she waited for us to eat. Everything's going to be fine, was her mantra for the week.

"Why can't we go see her?" asked Paulie.

"Your mother's tired, silly. She wants to rest a little. You'd be tired too if you had a baby."

Paulie looked skeptical. He'd been reading up on the subject and had begun to entertain suspicions. "I bet the cord got trapped around the neck," he whispered later, as we brushed our teeth. "That cuts off the oxygen, you know."

"Shut up, Paulie."

"Or maybe she had to have an operation. To get it out, I mean. That would take a long time to heal."

"Shut up, Paulie."

"That's what you always say. Shut up, Paulie. That's your answer for everything."

"Just shut up."

Possibly I had a greater influence on Paulie than I knew, because in the weeks that followed he hardly spoke at all. But then everyone in the family was a little distracted, because of the baby.

At first they didn't tell us anything was wrong, and we didn't ask. True, there was an odd flatness to the skull, and the eyes seemed wrong somehow, but I wasn't looking too closely—not at her, not at anything. My mind was a dull tool. If my father was right and adversity was a test of character, then already I could feel myself slumping back, closing the empty blue book. All I knew was that my wrist had betrayed me at a decisive moment, and as a result I would not be playing football that autumn, let alone proceeding to a brilliant professional career and the adoration of millions. None of that was going to happen. Knowing this, my ambitions did a quick one-eighty: I burned to be away, far away, college maybe, so that the rest of my life, my *alternative* life, whatever it was, could begin.

Oh, and I knew one more thing. I knew my parents were on the outs. And it had something to do with that little creature they'd brought back from the hospital.

There was one night in particular. Millie was in the kitchen, working double-time, chattering away like gunfire on the phone as she wrestled with a pot roast in the oven. My mother came into the dining room and fell into a chair, still chubby from being pregnant and bleary-eyed from no sleep. Her bathrobe was loose; through the folds I caught an unwanted glimpse of the forking, intricate blue veins in her stomach. I looked around for the baby but the baby was asleep in the bassinet. This, I had come to understand, was as much as you could hope for from babies.

Paulie was leafing through a magazine and nibbling a cracker. As a rule he had deplorable eating habits, my brother. He got away with it because of his ethereal thinness and pallor, his air of preoccupation with things higher than food. The less you appear to care about something, the more you get away with, in my opinion.

Outside it was still light.

My father came in and Paulie didn't look up when he sat down. "Put the magazine away," my father snapped. "We're having dinner."

"So?"

"So put the magazine away."

Very, very deliberately, Paulie folded up the magazine and placed it under his chair. The room was more than quiet. Either Millie had hung up the phone or else she was actually listening to someone else talk for a change. Or perhaps she was listening to us. Paulie's eyes were now locked on his plate, where the magazine had been, as if he was still reading in protest.

"What was so interesting?" I asked, just to get him talking.

"Yes," my mother said, looking at us for the first time. "Tell us, Paul. Tell us what's going on out there in the great wide world."

"How should I know?" He spat it out bitterly, as if we'd insulted him.

"You were the one with the magazine, shmuck," I reminded him.

"So?"

"So shut up."

"Both of you lower your voices," my father said. "You'll wake the baby."

At approximately this point in the party Millie waltzed in, bearing an enormous brisket in a covered pot. "I hope everybody's hungry," she said brightly. "I made a ton."

"I hate brisket," Paulie mumbled. "It's bad for you."

My father closed his eyes for a second. I had the feeling that he didn't care for brisket much either.

"It's Mom's recipe," Millie said, dishing out the meat with a slotted spoon. "I've never made it before."

"Which Mom?" Paulie asked in a mean voice. "Yours or mine?"

"I'm starved," I said quickly. Meaning shut up.

For a while, after she'd taken care of our plates, Millie seemed to lose all sense of purpose. Fluttering back and forth, she wiped her hands on her apron, went into the kitchen for some water, brought it to the table, then headed off again for something else. We were all waiting for her to sit down. Finally she came to a stop behind Paulie, leaning in so close to his face that their cheeks met. "Paul, honey, eat a little, okay? You're turning into a twig."

"I'm not a twig," said my brother, the literalist.

"Just a little, hon." I could see Millie trying to catch my mother's eye, to exchange a meaningful look, conspire together in this house of obstinate men. But my mother was looking pretty obstinate herself. "Just a bite, okay?"

Paulie shook his head.

"These boys," Millie sighed, affectionately—or half-affectionately anyway—mussing Paulie's hair. It was one of her least effective gestures.

"They're good kids," said my father, as if arguing with her.

"Oh they're treasures," she said. "Darlings. Sometimes when I look and see them all grown up like this I just know they can handle . . . I mean, if they *have* to—"

"Millie," my father broke in quietly.

For some reason this one rather benign mention of her name drove all the blood from Millie's face. She crumpled into her chair; it was as if she'd been tackled, I thought. No one spoke.

Paulie seized his chance. "Can I be excused?"

My father said no. My mother said okay. They spoke at the same time, then stopped and gazed across the table, almost curiously, as if each trusted the other must be right and was now waiting to hear why.

"I've got some stuff to do too," I said.

Finally my father let out his breath—apparently he'd been holding it—and looked down into the messy crevice of his baked potato. "You're both excused. Go have a good time." He didn't sound terribly optimistic about our chances of this, however.

After we left, the adults remained at the table, talking quietly among themselves, and the next morning Millie packed up her apron and went home. I rode with her to the train. Her perfume was all over my sinuses as I hugged her goodbye—more tightly, I think, than either of us expected—and so I was only vaguely aware of my father a few feet away, digging into his pocket to tip the redcap. "Be good, honey. And listen," she told me, "whatever happens, it'll be all right." Then my father came over to buss Millie on the cheek. He lingered a moment, whispering something into her impenetrable hairdo. "I know that," she said, her eyes unnaturally bright. "And I don't. I don't blame you at all."

I was sorry to see her go. This by itself seemed a bad sign.

Around this point summer session at the college let out, so my father now had time on his hands, too, waiting for the new term to start. He retreated into his study to read novels, drink iced coffee, and listen to music. Perhaps he was looking for excuses to get away from the baby, the sense of white, silent wrongness that attached to everything she did. Who could blame him? I was too.

One day when it was very hot we drove down to the shore. I couldn't swim with the cast on my wrist, but I waded out a few feet, picking up rocks and throwing them dopily at the waves, as if it mattered whether I hit them or not. Paulie, wearing a teeshirt to avoid sunburn, spent the whole time reading on the blanket. He didn't care for the beach. That was his position. He was a big one for not caring. My father, inspired by his example, swam for a while, made a halfhearted attempt to build a sand castle, and then gave up. For lunch he gave me a ten-dollar bill and told me to go over to the snack bar and buy whatever Paulie and I wanted. Then he lay down to take a nap.

It must have been a very short one, because a few minutes later, coming back with the food, I caught sight of him through the crowd, sitting on the blanket where I'd left him, staring vacantly ahead as he did an odd, wondrous, awful thing. He picked his nose. He was going at it savagely, making a pincer of two fingers, digging away like a miner. There was no way not to be revolted. While I was at it, I also happened to notice how weak his chin was, how his pale pancake of a chest had no hair, how despite his skinny legs and arms he carried an extra layer of flesh, like baby fat, that pooled and drooped at his hips, distorting the curve of his profile. It did not seem possible that this man was forty years old. Without his clothes he looked gawky and misshapen, like some overgrown kid. Like *me.* Immediately upon thinking this I wanted to run off and hide. But it was too late. He was right in front of me, looking up expectantly to see what sort of meal his money had bought.

"Hey," I said, and sat down on the blanket with the hot dogs. Paulie grunted but did not look up.

"Hey," he said. "How'd you make out?"

"No problem."

Just then a girl of about sixteen floated past us in a black bikini. I watched her for a second, dully thoughtful. Then I saw that my father was watching her too.

"What's her name going to be?" I asked.

"Hmm?"

"The baby. You guys going to name her, or what?"

He considered his knees for a moment, as if the answer was inscribed there.

"I just thought, you know, it's been a couple weeks now."

"Has it? Has it really?"

"Sure."

"You're right," he said. "But let's talk about it later, shall we? With your mother. Let's talk about it later with her."

• • •

And so that night they told us about the baby. It was after the dishes were cleared but before dessert, a time I normally enjoyed because it was so unstructured, so in-between, the day blurring itself out and the evening not yet settled firmly into place. They told us that the baby had a condition, a very serious condition, so serious that for the good of the family they had decided it was unfair to try to raise her at home, and that there was a good chance that by the time school started she would no longer be living with us but at a place set up to deal with Down's children, to give them a good—that is, a better—life, though of course she would always be our sister and we'd visit her at every opportunity and remain close to her somehow, even after we were grown. Altogether it required about ten minutes to explain the complexities.

When they were finished, they asked us for our opinions—my parents were nothing if not progressive—and I spoke up right away, saying that it didn't matter to me very much one way or the other, I just wanted everyone to be happy. Paulie waited until they turned and asked him specifically; then he said he felt the same way.

"Ah," said my mother, and nothing else. Her eyes in the dusk were luminous and still. She had slowed down enormously since the baby; she was no longer the same restless person. "Come here," she said.

She stooped over to hug us. Normally she was not very good at it. Her embraces were too tight, too fitful and bony. But now she felt softer, more yielding, less in a hurry to get up off her knees and do something else.

And yet, how do I say this? She wasn't quite there with us either. Her eyes were closed, her lips grimly pursed; she appeared to be taking more than she was giving. After a few seconds my father, who'd been standing a step behind her, waiting to hug us himself, gave up and went to the stove to make a pot of coffee. I watched him over my mother's shoulder as he stood peering into the empty filter. He looked impatient for all the explaining to be over and for Paulie and me to go to bed. I remembered the way he'd said goodbye to Millie, as though asking forgiveness. Now he looked tired of asking. Tired of the baby, tired of my mother, tired of all of us. It was perfectly obvious to me at that moment, with my mother's arms still cradling my back, who wanted what, and whose will had prevailed.

The next day my mother put on her good sundress, left the baby with my father, and spent the afternoon driving around to look at institutions. She was gone several hours. When she came back she poured herself a glass of white wine and settled into a corner of the couch to read. I asked her how it went and she gave a kind of low, dirty laugh I had never heard from her before. Then she opened the book.

She followed this same schedule three or four days in a row. We never offered to go along, and she never offered to take us.

On the fourth afternoon she was late getting started. None of her clothes seemed to fit quite right; she kept changing her mind and going back into the closet to start over. I was just hanging around, wondering what to do with myself as usual. For no good reason I asked if she wanted some company.

She frowned. "Sure you want to, kiddo?"

"I don't mind."

"School starts next week."

"So what?"

"So maybe you should take it easy. Enjoy your freedom."

I shrugged. By now it was obvious that freedom was wasted on me. I wasn't good at it. I couldn't execute. Freedom was just another crack I was slipping through.

"I don't mind," I said.

So we drove forty miles out to Nutley to look at a home. I

imagined it was a perfectly average home of that type, no worse than most, very clean, actually. Yes, I was inclined to give it the benefit of the doubt, and did so for, oh, about five minutes, before I started loathing the place. The floor had a sickly sheen, the walls were dull white, the corridors were full of echoes, quiet murmurs . . . it was like wandering through someone else's bad dream. Every adult who walked by seemed to be fighting the urge to break into a run. I didn't blame them. I was ready to run right out of there myself. But my mother was taking her time, dawdling in the doorways of the various rooms, asking questions. Then when the tour was over she stopped again in the main office, and embarked on a long, leisurely chat with the woman who worked there.

I sat out in the hallway on a plastic chair, waiting to leave. There were some pictures thumbtacked to the bulletin board and I looked them over. Each seemed designed to show off the entire spectrum of colors found in a Crayola box. There were blue mountains, yellow lakes, black trees, purple houses, orange fields. Having Down's, I thought, must be like a drug trip. Not that I had ever *taken* a drug trip, per se, but I had gleaned from some friends that one saw wonderfully strange and vivid colors when one was fucked up in that way. On the other hand, the drawings on that bulletin board were not so different from the birthday cards Paulie and I used to make for our parents when we were little. Possibly it was just being young that accounted for the distortions, made it so hard to see things, or present them, as they really were.

On our way out, some of the older kids waved at us from the window. Others just watched with vague, indifferent stares.

"So what do you think?" my mother asked as we climbed into the car.

"Me?" It hadn't occurred to me when I volunteered that my

opinion was going to be solicited. Now I cursed myself for not paying better attention while we were in there. "Hell, I don't know."

"They seemed happy," she said. She glanced down at her blouse, where some moisture stains had appeared that hadn't been there before. "It seemed like a good clean place."

"Right. It wasn't so bad."

"You should see some of the others. It would be pretty educational, I'll tell you that." She took a deep breath and began backing out of the parking lot. "Buckle yourself in, okay? I don't want to lose you."

I remembered, as we pulled away, a piece of information I might contribute to the decision-making progress. "Those pictures were pretty cool."

"What pictures?"

"The ones on the bulletin board. They were all colored and stuff. I mean, you don't draw pictures like that when you're unhappy."

This sounded rather feeble even to me. Also it did not upon reflection seem even remotely true. But my mother smiled. The sight encouraged me. She was bearing up pretty well, I thought. We both were. "Let's go home, kiddo. What do you say? Let's go make us some spaghetti."

That night we made spaghetti. We made meatballs. We made garlic bread. We made an enormous salad, and German chocolate cake for dessert. We made all this food and then as usual nobody but me ate it. My mother tried to hold on to her high spirits, chatting about little things, people she knew, stories in the paper, movies she wanted to see, all the things she had more or less stopped chatting about since the baby was born, and if there was anything forced or ungenuine about her that night I failed to notice. The baby was asleep in the back bedroom, so it was the four of us again. I was scarfing down the food; Paulie looked dreamy and irritable as he picked at his salad; my father had his head bent so far I could see through his hair to his scalp. And then my mother, still chirping away, tried to remember a joke she had heard from someone, Millie she thought, and when she arrived at the punchline my father lifted his head for the first time all night and stared at her wonderingly. It was as if even after all these years he could not believe how beautiful she was, with her long fine hair and her sloping blue eyes, and how extraordinary was his luck in being married to her.

But what he said was, "Please stop."

At once her face went white. Her lower lip began to tremble. "You stop," she said.

"Great." He pushed back his chair. "I'll stop. Okay?"

Nobody answered. It wasn't okay, clearly. Whatever okay was, this couldn't possibly be it. But who was going to tell him?

"Okay," he said. "So let's go." He looked around the table. "Who wants to go?"

"Where?" I asked.

"Wherever you want. I don't care. Putt-putt golf."

"No way." I held up my cast.

"Okay, a movie. What's at the Fox?"

"It's lousy. I saw it."

"Well then, how about bowling? You always liked bowling."

This was a fairly bizarre suggestion, coming from my father. He hated bowling. The whole atmosphere of the sport made him ill. On Saturday mornings, when I used to be in the league, he'd sit in the car with his coat on, smoking and correcting papers until I was finished.

"*I*'ll go," said Paulie, helping himself to some coconut slivers I'd picked off my cake.

I snickered. "You never bowled a game in your life, squirt."

"So what? Mr. Jackson says I have a lot of athletic potential."

"You?"

"I just need to develop it, he says."

"Paulie," I said, "you can develop all you want. You'll still have the potential of a retard."

It would be impossible to overstate how poorly this remark went over at our dinner table that evening. Everyone just stared at me with their mouths open, waiting for me to disappear.

"Okay." I threw my napkin down, disgusted with us all. "Let's go bowling."

The bowling alley was in the next town over, literally and figuratively across the tracks. We drove there with the windows down, all three of us in the front seat, listening to the syrupy ballads my father preferred when he was driving and gazing out at the moonless oddity of the night. We had not been out after dark in a long time. It was truly another world. We passed the White Castle where the cops hung out, and the Alibi Lounge with its blinking, leery sign. The parking lots were full; everyone was doing a lot of business. We had to circle around the bowling alley twice before a space opened up.

Inside, the cold air and the noise rushed forward to greet us. It was as if the place had been waiting for us to arrive, gathering up all its constituent parts—the light, the music, the hollow thunder of the pins, the girlish squeal of shoes on the polished floor—and putting them on display for our benefit. I had not been bowling in close to a year. There was a gaudy new carpet in the lobby, and a separate room laid out with arcade games in the back. The man at the register was also new. He was built like the football coaches at school: thick-armed, with small deep-set eyes and a squat, bulldog neck. He looked a little worn out from all the customers. A ballgame was playing on the TV behind him. He continued to keep his eye on it even as he came forward to deal with us.

"Excuse me," said my father. "We're going to need some shoes."

Grudgingly, the man handed us our shoes and a scoresheet.

"Wait." My father was confused. "Which lane do we go to?"

"Look on the sheet. It's right there on the sheet."

"It's not marked," my father said, looking over the sheet hopelessly as the man turned away.

"Hey Dad," I said. "Look, it's right here."

"That's not the point and you know it." He was glaring at the man's back. A muscle worked in his jaw. "He knows it too."

"Look," Paulie said, "they have Pepsi."

"Come on," I said to my father. "Who cares? Let's just bowl."

I am hard-pressed to account for our bowling that night. I had four or five strikes in the first game alone, and my father, my father was a revelation. He used to run the mile back in high school; he had those long, powerful legs with a lot of sinew in them, and when he whipped around on his hips and let fly with the ball it arced down the lane with a terrifying velocity. The pins, devastated, tumbled and spun. Everything he threw was on target. The first strike made him pump his fist and let out a yell—we all did—before he hid his face to conceal his satisfaction. Soon he stopped even trying to conceal it.

"I thought you hated bowling," I said.

"Not bowling. Just bowling alleys."

"What's so bad about bowling alleys?" Paulie asked. "They've got corn dogs and everything."

"It's the other bowlers I don't care for."

"Like us?" Paulie said. "We're other bowlers too."

"Don't flatter yourself," I said.

Actually Paulie was bowling pretty well, in his putzy, unpromising way. He was deficient in both form and force, but he had a good eye, and surprisingly nimble footwork. He threw fewer gutter balls than I would have expected. Once, I think, when I wasn't looking, he may have even pulled off a spare on a 7–10 split.

We bowled three games and did not want to stop. In the fourth game we played around cockily, doing little dance moves down the lane, making ridiculous bets. We were so involved in this way that we never noticed the snack bar shutting down, the lights clicking off in the neighboring alleys. I looked up at the clock; it was five to eleven. Suddenly I was aware of the surrounding darkness, of Paulie's high voice echoing around the cavernous room.

"I think they may be closing," I said.

My father was waiting for his ball to come up. "What round are we on?"

"Sixth."

He considered. "What about it, Paul? Want to finish this game, or call it a night?"

"I don't think there's time," I said.

Paulie drew himself up very straight. "If we started," he said, "we should finish."

So we played out the game. I was finding it difficult to concentrate on the score, however. In my mind's eye the whole building had turned against us, and we stood small and exposed in our narrow lane, spotlit in our frailty. The fact that I was the only one bothered by this did nothing to relax me.

Finally the game was over, and we changed back to our sneakers, gathered up our things, and headed toward the front desk.

When we laid our shoes on the counter, the clerk looked at them as if he had never seen bowling shoes before. It was the same man we had dealt with on the way in. His eyes, if possible, were even smaller, deeper, and harder. The TV in the corner was now off. I knew then that he'd been wanting to close up for a while and blamed us for being so slow.

As I say, *I* knew it; exactly what plane of perception my father and brother were inhabiting was anyone's guess. Even now they continued to joke around, comparing scores, promising rematches the next week. I had to nudge my father just to get him to pay. And then I saw him reach for the checkbook, and I knew right away that we were in for it.

"We don't take checks," the clerk said through his teeth. He had waited until my father finished signing his name to tell us.

"It's local," my father said. "Are you sure?"

"We don't take checks."

"Fine, you don't take checks. Here—" he was still making a joke of it, or pretending to, as he took out his wallet, "look, no problem, I'll give you the cash I have. I'm a bit short . . . four twenty-five, four fifty . . . okay, I owe you, what, six and a half bucks . . . call it seven. I'll drop it in the mail tomorrow."

The bulldog just shook his head. He had a kind of nasty inner gravity that seemed to emanate from his chest and exert itself upon us all. I felt my own head begin to shake in syncopation with his.

"Alright then. Why don't you just take my check and we can all go home."

"We don't want your fucking check. I just told you."

"Watch your language, please," my father said heatedly. "These are children here."

"I don't care what they are."

I heard Paulie beside me, drawing a loud breath. The hairs on the back of my neck had begun to tingle.

"You've got no consideration, playing all night when I'm trying to close. Now you can't pay. What is it with you people? What are you trying to pull?"

There was something in "you people" that took what was happening out of the realm of the strictly personal and made me conscious, as I rarely was in those days, of the curliness of our hair and the bone structure of our noses. But perhaps all he meant was the usual meaning—that is, everyone who wasn't him. We had no time to decode it. He was taking a step toward my father, and my father, thin hands trembling, was taking a step toward him. They were going to fight. They were going to fight, and my father—there was no doubt in my mind—was going to get his ass kicked, and there was nothing to be done to stop it. Paulie was wobbling around beside me, staring at the television, waiting for it to come on again and envelop us in its familiar glow. But we were out here now, in the dumb, accidental world. Out here, things piled up around you with a brutish, oceanic logic, and no sooner had you got one of them behind you than another loomed in front, and somehow this had transpired in such a way that we were now forced to watch our father get his ass kicked by some idiot in a bowling alley for no particular reason; the same no particular reason, I thought wildly, that had given us the baby, who was lying in the crib at home right now with her slanty eyes and flat nose and her lousy, accidental future. And then I couldn't help it, all the rages of the summer came spewing out.

Get away from me! Get away from me goddamn you!

According to Paulie, who is not entirely to be trusted in these matters, I was screaming so insanely he could hardly make out the words, so it wasn't clear who I meant to get away from me, and why. Apparently I wedged myself between the two men, and shoved. The strange part was this: the person I shoved was not the bulldog, but my father. I shoved him really hard. I threw myself at him, buried my face in his solar plexus, heaving up from below as if charging a tackling dummy, and then kept pounding him backwards toward the door. "Okay, okay," he said, giving ground. *"Okay."*

But my execution, and his lack of resistance to it, was so gratifying, so personally rewarding, that I kept on pounding him, even after we were out the door, Paulie trailing anxiously behind us, even after we were out on the sidewalk that led to the parking lot, even after we were only a few short yards from the car. I kept pounding. I was perfectly capable of pounding him the entire way home. But then he stiffened. He shook his head quizzically, as if waking from a dream, and a red sun dawned in his eyes, and before I knew it he was shoving me back. It must have felt gratifying to him too. He grabbed me in a bear hug and shook me until my eyes blurred. Poor Paulie kept whimpering for us to stop. It was beginning to seem like a good idea to me. I was almost overcome by the immediacy of the man, the rankness of his sweat, the proximity of his organs below his clothes—I could feel one of his arteries pounding away at me—and a raw, terrible sound I heard, though I don't think he did, lodged deep in his throat. Still, I held on. I had a host of grudges to fuel me. If before I'd been angered by his weakness, now I was angered by his strength, a strength I'd somehow misread, it seemed, as I'd misread so many other things that summer. So we kept at it, thrashing and bumping against the car like an enraged two-headed moth, not really getting anywhere at this point—for my part, I was no longer trying to—but as if under the grip of some awful species compulsion. At last the old man grew cunning, reared up trickily from the hips; with one hand free, he lifted it high to swat me—

And that was when he faltered. Maybe his hand remembered that it was full of the same blood as my own, and that was why it hung for a moment, half-open, half-closed, in midair. Who knew? Who cared? By now I had slipped sentiment's leash. Almost without thinking (but not quite, not quite without thinking) I hopped quickly sideways, raised my cast, and brought it down with all my weight on the side of his head.

He let go of me, then.

He didn't fall, but stumbled back against the front fender, where he remained in a crouch, gingerly feeling his scalp with the palm of his hand. I backed away. The punch I'd thrown, if that's what it was, hadn't satisfied me; I still felt capable of throwing more. I went over to the passenger's side and jerked the door open, prepared to punch that too if necessary.

Immediately upon sitting down, all my strength deserted me. I leaned my head against the seat and closed my eyes. In the distance trucks were shifting gears, climbing the on-ramp to the parkway. I could all but taste their exhaust in my mouth.

At last my father got up, climbed stiffly into the driver's seat, and lit a cigarette. He exhaled wearily, looking around. "Where's your brother?"

"Right there."

I nodded toward the sidewalk, where Paulie was marching back and forth like a toy soldier, petulantly kicking gravel with his sneakers. He knew we were waiting, but I suppose he too wished to register his unhappiness that night. Anyway my father didn't seem to mind. He sat there smoking. In the glow of the streetlamp his hands were like x-rays. Just a few spindly bones.

Then I had an idea.

"You're the one, aren't you? You're the one that wants to keep her."

I was remembering Millie's goodbye: "I don't blame *you.*"

"Look, just tell me, okay? It doesn't matter. I just want to know."

"Know *what*?" His mouth was twisted, contorted. "Know *what*?"

"You know," I said vaguely. "Everything."

He laughed. The sound was private and bitter, even a little dirty, the same way my mother's had been that time she came back from the first institution. Knowing things they didn't care to know, it appeared to give them a quiet, transient pleasure, an acrid taste on their tongue they both savored and regretted, like cigarette smoke, and then finally expelled. To me it gave no pleasure at all. My father was through with me now, so I turned to watch my brother through the windshield, hands jammed into his pockets, slouching moodily against the hood of the car. It used to cheer me up sometimes to consider how different we were, Paulie and I, to take inventory of those differences and be glad that I wasn't him. But now I didn't feel that way. I was uncertain about where and how to draw the lines between us, or if there were even lines to be drawn. In a week, high school would start, and the uncertainty, I knew, would only accelerate. The skin under my cast had begun to itch. I felt it all the way up in my head.

Finally Paulie opened the door behind me and slid into the back seat. He was tired, he said. He wanted to go home.

My father remained quiet, lost in thought.

"Hey," said Paulie, leaning between us. "What're we waiting for?"

"Shut up," I said. "We'll be there soon."

Between Hammers

Rennie is singing.

We're in bed, it's late, we've had a rotten week, stubbled with disappointments, and what I want to say is that nothing is inevitable, nothing fully known. I want to tell Rennie this but she happens to be asleep at the moment, curled into a C with her back to me. She sings in her sleep, Rennie. It's something she does. Of course there are worse things a wife could do in her sleep. She could snore, or scream, or have sex with the doorman. A little singing, what's that? I like music as much as anybody.

When we first began going together, I would try to hum along. It seemed a unique opportunity to bond. I was in my twenties then and given to obscure, severe prejudices and habits; for example, I had difficulty sleeping in any bed softer than my own. Rennie's bed in particular was a trial—a plump, massive, boxspringed affair—so I was usually up anyway, staring at the ceiling, when her night music started. But my humming appeared to irritate Rennie, to break up the rhythm she had established over the years of solo sleeping, and force it to accommodate to mine. So I learned to keep quiet, to listen and to not listen, both at once.

This was not an unusual strategy around Rennie. I first put it into practice the night we met, at an otherwise boringly congenial dinner party in Park Slope. We were seated across from each other, so I had an unobstructed view of her manners and mannerisms, her whole variegated repertoire of tense, fidgety expressions. Let's give Rennie credit: she didn't like me any better than she liked anyone else in the room. Her dislike was so acute and explicit, in fact, that it required an enormous failure of sensitivity on my part, the very thing she already didn't like about me, to approach her at the end of the evening, as I did, and invite her out. All I knew of women was their mercuriality, and in this respect Rennie did not disappoint me, not then and not in the months of courtship that followed. She was a big pale freckled blonde with a brisk, imperious manner, a manner she tried to offset by speaking very softly and by a certain languid approach to cigarette smoking. In truth the nicotine made her jittery, and the many theatrical gestures that accompanied its intake—the soaring sky-jets of smoke, the violent squashing of butts—only made her look difficult, self-involved. I found her at once utterly compelling and potentially rather tiresome. Perhaps she found me the same way. For a long time we saw each other only on Friday nights, after her swim at the Y. But then gradually we began to spend weekends together in the airy apartment she'd inherited from her mother, with the same slipcovered furniture she'd grown up with and the same slender views of Riverside Park from three different rooms.

I remember coming into it that first night, standing there at the open window, looking out at the low, bumpy darkness of Jersey and listening to the night sounds well up through the foliage while Rennie went about her business, hanging up her swimsuit and playing back her messages and going through the mail, as though she were quite alone. Then at some point she seemed to recall why I was there; she lit a candle, and we made love, and afterwards she collapsed heavily into sleep, her hair still damp and smelling of chlorine, and the music of her inmost organs floated up through her throat-pipes—thin, tuneless, meandering, and yet as incontestably timeless and compelling as the jingle of the ice cream truck that swings by on summer evenings between eight and nine, summoning the children of the neighborhood.

Rennie's songs are a summons, too, though even now I do not know of whom or for what. She does not know either. Whenever I mention that I heard her singing in her sleep she narrows her lids at me and puffs out her cheeks, two of her many gestures of dismissal.

In a way I feel sorry for Rennie. She's been so long a skeptic that she is unable to stop being skeptical, even on those rare occasions skepticism isn't called for. It's a problem with people who have had a great deal of hardship in their lives and who now fancy themselves survivors. This survivalism becomes a kind of license they brandish when pulled over to account for selfish behavior. For years I prized her narrow-gazed obstinacy, came to depend upon it as a leash for my many wayward and unruly enthusiasms. But lately I'm not so sure. Lately Rennie's attitude strikes me as a mere reflexive posture, something wearying and formidable and ultimately dull.

Now Rennie moves, and her breath cuts short; I hear a little swallow. It might be that she's about to wake and head off to the kitchen for a glass of water—singing is thirsty work—or it may be a pivot point, a curve in her sleep's road which will lead her back to me. I shift my weight, open my arms to receive her. Every night is a potential beginning.

But she doesn't wake. She mumbles foggily and clutches her pillow to her chest, or perhaps lower. In no time at all she has resumed her even breathing. Then there it is again, her song, murmuring like a brook over the sand and stones of her preoccupations, and I'm alone again, all ears and arms and a mouthful of undelivered messages.

Rennie teaches expository writing at a college out in Queens. It's fair to say she's underemployed. She has a Ph.D. in Comparative Literature from NYU and a book of translations forthcoming—German poetry—from a university press on the West Coast. The book, which holds the key to her career advancement, has been held up in production for reasons no one has quite been able to identify. Once a month Rennie sends the editor a note, politely reminding him that she has yet to receive her galleys, and once every six months or so she gets a note back appealing to Rennie for patience in the matter. Each note comes from a different editor, or possibly a succession of people in the same editorial position, because in all likelihood people who work at university presses are no happier or more stable in their jobs than are people who work at community colleges. "They probably leave when they get pregnant," says Rennie. "That's the way it happens with these people."

Who are these people, I'm wondering. Are we these people, or are we other people? We're still not quite sure, Rennie and I, what kind of people we are.

As for me, I'm what you might call a bioengineer. I do design and development for the orthopedics division of a pharmaceutical company across the river. My specialty is prosthetic systems, knees and hips, mostly. Though it was not my first choice for a career—neither my grades nor motivation were high enough for medical school—it is a demanding one, requiring a precision and imagination that seem to me fully the equal of medicine, or for that matter German poetry. Rennie might argue the point. I almost wish she would. But like many unhappy people she lacks the energy for debate, the curiosity for other views. She no longer asks me about the problems I wrestle with all day—the shrinkage factors, the CAD/CAM glitches, the polymer fatigue. She has shrinkages and glitches and fatigues of her own.

Rennie, I want to say, take on a new project. We are shaped by what we do, as well as what we don't do; there's no neutral ground, no wisdom in the waiting life. But even poetry, *especially* poetry, has lost its urgency for her.

At first we figured it must be me. It had been over a year, and though we surely knew enough to get ourselves checked, neither of us really wanted to. We tried for a few more months on our own. We understood ourselves to be capable people, young and resilient enough to work it through, presuming we could identify what it was. Occasionally we'd lie on our respective pillows, Rennie smoking, me looking over a design, and speculate—sometimes aloud, sometimes not—about the unseen factors involved. I'd think of the food, the water, the snug fit of my undershorts, the microwave oven at the restaurant I worked for back in college. The porousness of membranes, the impurities in the air. How can one live in this metallic age and remain inviolate? Remain whole? Still, people do. We know that; we meet them in the park every day. So when Rennie says let's try a little longer, we try a little longer.

• • •

At work there is a growing demand for kneecaps and shoulder sockets, critical hinges. We're all overworked. Seven hundred Dominicans and Puerto Ricans in the manufacturing division are at time and a half, and still we can't keep pace.

Which does not prevent my supervisor, Eddie Gramm, a man as lacking in charisma and purpose as any I've met, from passing afternoons in my cubicle, fondling my prototypes and dispensing uncharitable judgments. "You're lucky to have a wife at all," he says. "You should see what it's like out there for the solo artist. Tough to get a long-term contract."

"There's always losing yourself in your work," I say pointedly.

"Work," Eddie grunts.

"People are crying out for assistance, Eddie."

"Exactly. That's what I told them upstairs. Let's stop fucking around with the small stuff and get into whole-body design. There's money in that."

At night I return home to a wordless, alcohol-free dinner, to reading and television and a view out the living room window of the clustered boats in the Seventy-ninth Street Basin, nodding their heads to the commands of the current, and then we go to bed, Rennie and I, and commence our labors. Sex is a kind of construction project. A joint probe into space. It is as intricate and practical as the launch of a rocket, and yet like a rocket there is something almost inconceivable about it, something too large to wrap our minds around. There are hurried countdowns, awesome trajectories, garbled transmissions. We bound across craters, slip through Saturn's rings. When we finally splash down it is to an expectant earth, one that clamors for results, for photo opportunities, banner headlines. We duck our heads and retreat to someplace quiet for debriefing.

Our heart survives between hammers. I found that in one of Rennie's poetry books, translated from the German. The line pops into my head occasionally on these long nights after splashdown. I would like to explore its meaning with Rennie but invariably she has fallen asleep, her soft, wheezing song already tickling my shoulder.

Sometimes, lying here in the half-light listening to Rennie, I'll pick up some of the student essays she leaves on the nightstand under her glasses. As a rule they are badly typed, on curling recycled paper that smells of smoke (Rennie's), but sometimes in the sloppiness and secondhandedness there is a kind of charming sincerity, a willingness to commit, to throw language at the world's wall and see what sticks.

There are a great many essays about abortion, capital punishment, euthanasia, stem cell research. Her students appear to be obsessed with these issues.

Aziz Hassan has titled his argument paper "*IS VIOLINS EVER JUSTIFIED?*"

Ramon Rivera writes about soccer. His personal narrative essays are about soccer, his argument essays are about soccer, his critical analysis papers are about soccer. Rennie has been teaching him for two semesters now and can't get him to write about anything else. Either despite or because of this he is one of her favorite students.

I read through Ramon's latest soccer opus, which is pretty good, and then pick up the paper about violins being justified, discovering the author to be of two minds on the subject, as are we all.

It turns out that it isn't me, it's Rennie.

A new doctor tells us this one Friday afternoon. He's as young as I am and for a moment when he gives us the news I sense a vague complicity between us, as though we're both secretly relieved to have finally found something our gender can't be blamed for. His name is Hoffman. He's thin and handsome and wears no wedding ring, and so all at once I am absurdly jealous of him and wonder if in fact he isn't flirting with Rennie. The way he touches her just above the elbow. His low, reassuring murmur of a voice. I know how doctors operate, so to speak. This one's as smooth as any I've seen. He is speaking to her with somber intensity about dye tests and sonograms, and she leans forward and nods the way she always does with strangers and only rarely does with me. All her briskness has fled with the news. She exhales a long breath. Her hands seek refuge under her thighs. She looks like a schoolgirl receiving a quiet reprimand from a favorite teacher.

Hoffman outlines the tests he intends to run in the weeks ahead. He cocks an eyebrow at me to see if I'm paying attention or worrying about money or what. "No problem," I hear myself say, not all that forcefully.

"Right," chirps Rennie, getting to her feet. "No problem." She repeats the phrase five or six times on our way out of his office, smiling so fixedly that the next couple, rising off the sofa in the waiting lounge for their own appointment, begin to smile too. We move past each other, all lunatic smiles, as if the four of us are teammates in some elaborate relay race for the innocent.

It seems there is a blockage.

Rennie's depression deepens. I do my best to soothe her but my best, let's face it, is rarely equal to that task. In her cranky self-absorption she begins to remind me of my grandfather, a brainy, arrogant person who did not mind letting us all know, as his powers diminished, just how unhelpful and inadequate we were.

He used to lie there in the hospital looking up from the depths of his rage, clear-eyed, skin a jaundiced yellow, mouth crinkled in distaste from the assault of the tubes, and under his unblinking stare I heard myself make any number of foolish statements about myself and Rennie and my job, going on at great length, as people do when there is no one to stop them. When I finished he'd lift his wrist to look at his watch. Then he'd wave me away, refusing to console me for my failure to console him. In fact he appeared to blame me for it.

Occasionally on the ride home from the clinic I'll say something comic or hopeful to Rennie and she'll look down and I'll imagine that she too is looking at her watch the same way my grandfather, that son of a bitch, did before he died.

It's hot out now and since Rennie objects to air conditioning for some reason we make do with a fan, the windows open wide enough to admit every siren, scream, and horn blast in the borough. Rennie sits up in bed, grading essays; she scribbles furiously in the margins, grunting occasionally from pleasure or disbelief when something surprises her. Not much does. I've had an exhausting week and the last thing I feel like doing is making love to my unhappy, hormone-ravaged wife, but that is in fact what I am lying there waiting to do.

This is prime time, Hoffman told us the day before. He was taking a sonogram, waving his magic wand. He showed it all to me on the screen. That shadow was Rennie's bowel, that one her intestine, that one the bladder; and there, those troublesome oblongs, her ovaries with their shadowy follicles. Here was the outer Rennie lying on the table, watchful and silent, while Hoffman and I hovered above, charting her insides like cartographers—pointing fingers, plotting strategies, discussing data, doing our male business. It gave me an odd sense of peace. Apparently, though Hoffman and I work with different anatomies, our methods are similar. Watching him print out his designs, I thought, how gratifying to be standing here with technology and the insight it affords, with people who can do with machines what would otherwise not be done. When the sonogram was over he advised us to have relations as often as possible in the coming week and we assured him, as has become our habit, that this was no problem. Then on our way out of the office, Rennie reached for a cigarette, and I made a remark, and in the thirty hours since we have spoken very little.

Now she sighs significantly and takes off her reading glasses. "I shouldn't have gone into poetry," she says. "If only I had the courage to pursue my ultimate dream."

"Which is?"

"Hotel administration."

I laugh, happy to have provided her with a straight line, to be working together in the vaudeville act of a successful marriage. I reach for her but she has already moved to switch off the light. When she turns back in bed she has a cigarette lit. The red tip glows like a traffic signal on a dark street.

"I never go swimming anymore," she says, with the petulant vehemence she reserves for non sequiturs.

"Why not?"

"There's no time. There's just no time for anything."

"Time is something you make," I say pedantically. Rennie is beginning to really annoy me. "Besides, this is nothing. If you think there's no time now, just wait until we . . . until there's a—"

"I know," she says. "I know."

"Speaking of which—"

"I *know*!" Gathering her weight forward, she begins to rock herself, arms around her knees, as if about to perform a cannonball into an invisible pool below the bed. It takes a second or two before I discover that she's crying. A wave of forgiveness breaks in my chest. The drugs, I think, the drugs and the stress and the indignities of the clinic and the loss of control over her most private chemistry. Who wouldn't be erratic? Who wouldn't complain?

My grandfather, all those months, looking at his watch.

"Rennie," I say softly, "if we don't want to, we don't have to."

Wiping her nose on her knee, she says, "I don't want to."

"No problem."

"Don't say no problem. If there's one thing I'm not in the mood to hear, it's no problem."

"Okay, sure, no problem," I say, at a loss. Maybe I'm trying to drive her crazy now, I don't know. I have a terrible impulse to pound the wall, smash the window. The world is full of blockages I can't break through. Rennie stretches out with her back to me and it takes everything I have not to punch her right in the spine.

Is violins ever justified?

A minute later I hear it, her faint, rhythmic singing. For the first time in our history together it occurs to me that people just don't sing in their sleep. Rennie must be faking, I think, must have always been faking. I bend over her like a detective, very close, inspecting the slope of her face for evidence.

But apparently people just do sing in their sleep, or at least Rennie just does, because no matter how long I watch her this way, with full vigilance and distrust, she continues to sing, and breathe evenly, and not move, and the trembling that seizes her from time to time is only the kind we all undergo nightly, the involuntary spasms of the body in its rest.

• • •

The next morning I'm walking past the playground in Riverside Park, where the children are chasing each other in circles, and I see a young girl, dark and olive-skinned, trip over someone's leg and hurt her knee. I watch the whole drama play out across her face: the fall, the moment of shock, the dawning recognition that yes, this is pain, this is bad, this is *really* bad. No one rushes to help her. She begins to cry.

In seconds I'm on my knees in front of her, telling her everything will be fine. "I'll go get your mother," I say.

"No, don't."

"Why not?"

"I'm crying," she announces, though this is no longer strictly true.

"It's because you fell and hurt your knee."

"Is it all better?" she asks, looking me over warily.

"Let me see."

From a respectful distance I examine her knee. There is a small discolored bruise on the cap, though whether from this fall or a previous one I can't be certain. She has, I notice, an externally rotated tibia, a slightly low-riding patella, and an impressive range of motion. I have done a lot of work with knees, but never, it seems, have I looked at a knee as intently as I am looking at this one. If only Rennie could see it too, this soft and perfect and resilient design.

"All better?" she asks again, a little impatient now to get on with things.

"All better. Only next time you sh—"

But she has already fled back to the sandbox, without so much as a limp.

• • •

Dye tests, Clomid, HCG. Endometrial biopsies.

Hoffman asks us not to go away in August so he can monitor Rennie's progress under Pergonal.

Rennie is teaching summer school. She has some hard days with it. It is a hard day when she gets her period, of course, and then for several days after, and a great many other days too.

Another note arrives from the university press. It says that all the production delays have been worked through; Rennie's book is now scheduled for the spring list. A small check is soon to follow.

She reads the note over Chinese food we've reheated from the night before. Her face is flushed and freckled with sweat. Lately we've been too hot to cook, and have taken to ordering an enormous quantity of Chinese food on Monday nights, which we live off of the rest of the week.

"How stupid do they think I am?" she asks, tossing her hair. "Do they really expect me to fall for this shit again?"

"This time sounds different," I say, though in fact it does not sound very different. I have made up my mind, though, to feel differently about it. "This time's for real."

"Right."

"Rennie," I say, "why not decide it's for real? Just decide it's for real and see what happens."

She puffs out her cheeks. "If there's one thing I don't need, it's another guru."

Now we are furious with each other all over again, so angry neither of us dares say a word. It takes a long time to get past it. We finish the dishes and retreat to separate corners for a while, and then much later, having delayed as long as we can, we go to bed, where without speaking or kissing or foreplay or any intimations of tenderness we have the relations as ordered by Dr. Hoffman, whom I picture whizzing through Larchmont in his golden Saab, dispensing pills that dissolve sweetly on the tongue, syringes full of magical fluids.

Two weeks later the check from Rennie's publisher has arrived, and her period, so mercilessly punctual all these months, has not.

It takes some getting used to, these new arrivals, new departures. Neither of us is as comfortable with change as we would like to believe. Perhaps no one is.

Tonight, however, we go out to dinner. There's a quiet, unexpected pleasure in saying no to the wine and yes to the appetizers, the heavy entrées, the elaborate desserts. When we come home we get into bed rather shyly, and because we're terribly full we don't make love even though for a change we sort of want to. Instead we cuddle close, and Rennie falls asleep even quicker than usual, her arms wrapped around my waist, her mouth against the back of my neck. A cool breeze comes in off the river and for a moment it feels like the same thing, the breeze and Rennie's breath, all moist and salty from nearby oceans. Tonight I too will fall asleep quickly. I know, because tonight of all nights Rennie is silent. I believe she is in shock, Rennie. I believe she is, in a sense, almost disappointed by this wonderful turn of events—because she could not see it coming, because the only difference between this week and last week is that some mechanism of production which was not working properly might have finally come around. And because she does not believe, as I do, that there are harmonious designs in nature which are invisible but not absent, it all seems somehow superstitious to her; she can't bring herself to trust it. It could slip away. There is a distinct statistical possibility it could slip away. And should this happen, what else may slip away with it?

And now I feel her weight against me, and her moist breath in my ear, and I remember, my god, how she used to look on Friday nights, her skin all pink from the shower at the Y, a big blond girl fresh from swimming. Of course, that was before—before we lived together, before we married, before the cooking and the laundry and the trips to Nova Scotia in rental cars that were never quite so nice as we planned. That was before my grandfather died; before I replaced my first hip; before I saw the shadows of Rennie's internal organs on that black, humming screen. I knew only surfaces then. I was as limited and stubborn in my way as Ramon Rivera, her bard of soccer. But I remain with Rennie, as Ramon does, because she too is stubborn, because love requires us to stubbornly imperil each other, to demand that which can't be given, and to go on demanding it. Every romance is a war of philosophies; the stakes are the romance itself. And if one person wins, it's all over.

And now here I go, drifting off. There's music playing somewhere, in one of the neighboring apartments, probably. It's an odd, slow song, one I've heard before, one which I'm sure I could pin down if it were in any way important to do so. But I'm not going to try. I'm going to fall asleep thinking it's Rennie, because Rennie is who it usually is.

Influence

I

I'd like to think this is my story, more or less.

Allow me to put forth the proposition that my motives where Elgin was concerned were selfless ones. I invited him to read here at the college because it seemed to me the right thing to do. Let's presume for argument's sake that I know the difference between the right thing to do and the wrong thing to do—though the opposite could be argued, and has been, by Laura among others—and am roughly capable of choosing among them. Can we move on?

In a small way I wanted to honor the man. That's what I told myself on the drive to the airport. I had a book coming out and I was feeling magnanimous; I wanted to do somebody a good turn. And Elgin was the one. Because whatever else you might say about Elgin Ricks—and I have a great deal to say about him—he was worthy of special treatment. Not a major figure perhaps, not a lasting one, but he'd had, in his time, a stature. A force. Ask Laura. I'm not the only one of his students who'd been secretly infatuated with the man, who'd learned to see and inhabit the world Elgin's way, with Elgin's loathing and wit, his fierce, arrhythmic music. Ask Laura. Eighteen years later, we still heard his voice in our heads, fretful and insinuating; still saw his winged shadow, a big bird on the radar screen, the brilliant sinewy angel whom we'd wrestle beneath the stars of our dreams. Let's leave aside the whole issue of father surrogates, of stern, withholding authority figures one seeks forever to please. Let's not pretend to understand. There's too much understanding already, too much easy analysis. What good does it do? *We must learn to love the difficult.*

That's Elgin's line, of course. I trot it out for my students from time to time. The brighter ones, like Valerie Ruane, they're fond of such remarks. They seem to feel it's just what they came to college for, this sort of taxing and paradoxical expression. Of course they don't know it's not my line but Elgin's, or rather not Elgin's per se but Rilke's, or rather Elgin's version of Rilke, or rather my own version of Elgin's version of Rilke—and god alone knows where Rilke's version of Rilke came from. The shameful ploys of the teaching profession are well known; there's no need to document them here. There isn't space or time. I am trying to tell the story of Elgin's visit, even if so far, let's face it, I'm doing a pretty poor job. What would Elgin have said about an opening as slow as this one? *Enough with the throat-clearing! Get going!*

Sometimes it's more than I can bear, writing stories, or for that matter reading them. All this heavy furniture to be lifted, these clinging, tiresome moralities to be dispensed. Why must events be given shape? There's a considerable pressure involved, just getting started. That is, if you can *get* started. And in this case I have my doubts.

Every story goes wrong, Elgin used to tell us. To report this gave him pleasure, a mature, acrid satisfaction, like the taste of espresso, or the darkest possible chocolate. Clearly going wrong was a good thing, in Elgin's view. Clearly going wrong, in Elgin's view, was the very nature of the story-writing project: the vessel, the target, the slow-burning fuel. Sooner or later, in Elgin's view, every story lost its way, arrived in a place it didn't know it was headed, and the best you could hope for was an honest account of this misfortune, the abandoned map of your doomed and wayward expedition. Like marriage. The metaphor was Elgin's, not mine, though Laura might claim otherwise. You'd have to ask her.

Speaking of vessels and targets, I was, you may recall, on my way to the airport to fetch Elgin Ricks. Who else would do it? Ours was a small liberal arts college; I had no graduate assistants on whom to dump such an errand. My department chair, Stanley Baldridge, whose influence with the dean had paved the way for Elgin's visit, was exceptional among my colleagues for being amiably disposed to living writers, occasionally even to the point of reading them; on the other hand he was also, perhaps incidentally, an alcoholic, and not to be trusted behind the wheel in the late afternoon. So I was the one. The airport was down in Hamilton, a two-and-a-half-hour drive in a good car. And I did not own a good car. I owned a bad car—an '89 Dodge with leaky hoses, underachieving shocks, and a rather piecemeal and desultory approach to internal combustion. I had bought the thing used from a student at the college, who has since gone on to business school at NYU while I of course have remained up here in the provinces, driving his malodorous machine. Never mind. Never mind the clan of intrepid, upwardly mobile mice who had gentrified the heating system, so when I turned on the fan I was greeted by a cheerful feathery turd-scented spray of decomposing nests. Never mind the trapezoidal gash in the floor, through which

I was able to see the highway spool by, gray and pitted, like an old movie. I diverted myself by thinking about the car I would buy if tenure came through, as I had every reason to expect it would. I had a good record, strong evaluations from the students, and few enemies I knew of among my colleagues. True, I had few friends among them either. How could I? For years I had arranged my schedule in such a way that I hardly saw them. I wrote stories in the mornings, I played with my children in the afternoons, and though the college would have preferred otherwise I taught my classes at night, and so by now I'd achieved an all but seamless and comprehensive detachment from the place, from the noisy daylight affairs of the academic mind. No wonder I was so lonely. No wonder I'd been looking forward to Elgin's visit for the past eight months.

Then too I had the new book coming out, the novel, for which I entertained higher than the usual hopes. I had an advance less shameful than most. I had testimonial blurbs from several authors, prominent ones, among them Elgin Ricks. *This guy might be the real thing.* Only seven words—Elgin was famously terse with praise—but after eighteen years they felt like fireworks. In a fever of vindication I'd written the man a letter of extravagant thanks, invited him to come read at the college, name your price. We had a ridiculously large endowment for such purposes, and the usual quotient of bright, melancholic student writers in need of consolation. Nonetheless I was pretty sure he wouldn't come.

For the main thing about Elgin at this point was this: he had not been seen in print in several years. He had not been seen much *out* of print either. It was something we all talked about. Friends would visit us for the weekend—yes, even up here in the sticks, where the trains run once a day—old friends from college with their midlife hungers and nostalgias, their overly attended-to children and their shopping bags full of expensive urban treats, and inevitably at a certain point in the evening, after the kids and the dishes were tucked away and the third bottle of wine had breathed its last, someone would say, "have you heard?" and off we'd go, falling into the kind of winsome tabloid haze people like Elgin always seem to inspire among people like us—he'd stopped writing, he'd quit teaching, he'd remarried Louise, he was polishing a screenplay about the life of Celine, he'd remarried Janet, he'd abandoned a thousand-page novel about the IRT, he'd moved down to Oaxaca with his daughter's Spanish teacher, or his Spanish teacher's daughter . . . What difference did it make? He was out there somewhere, performing the great play of his life, while we sprawled before the flickering fire, watching the shadows dance. He was our Hendrix, our Elvis, our UFO. A streak across the sky, got everyone talking and pointing, and now you couldn't find his books in the stores. Not even the third one, the stunner, the book we'd fed on over and over, the words trickling through our veins like an IV drip. You couldn't just walk in and buy it. You had to get on the computer and run a search.

But now he was coming. Now he was mine.

Like many of my colleagues I find it pleasant and purposeful, when driving a long distance, to occupy my mind with a book on tape. That afternoon I was listening to *Macbeth.* Though it was difficult, with the blasting of the heater and the low thrumming of the snow tires and the querulous honking of the geese overhead, to make out all the lines. *Your face, my thane, is as a book where* something *may read* something . . . *He that's coming must be provided* something something . . . *you shall put* something *into* something . . . It was at approximately this point that I looked down at the steering wheel and saw my hands were trembling. Why, I wondered, were they always so complicated and nervous-making, these human visitations? Perhaps Elgin's opinion (of me) mattered (to me) too much. That was Laura's view, and Laura could speak to the question with some authority. She was there at the beginning, in the front row of Elgin's class, skinny, watchful, in frayed jeans and Guatemalan peasant blouse, jotting down arresting phrases in her notebook with the Mont Blanc pen her parents, who were anything but Guatemalan peasants, had given her for Christmas. She used to write her stories with that pen too. Longhand. They were good stories, serious, formally ambitious, highly promising as undergraduates go. Even Elgin had said so, and he'd rarely said that of anyone—he certainly never said that of mine—but now it's been many years since she employed that pen for that purpose and the whole idea of promising stories has become a rather tender subject for Laura. It's what we who have logged our share of hours in marriage counseling call an "issue." Of course there are others, other "issues." Ask Laura. She'll be happy to tell you what they are.

Finally I arrived at the airport. Snow was tickling the windshield, harmless and light. I parked in the short-term lot and headed toward the terminal. The glass doors sighed open and closed. Inside, the counters were thronged. People were lugging their baggage toward the gates, lining up stoically at the security machines, prisoners of travel, emptying their pockets, submitting to the waves and probes of the electric wands. Such hard work, getting free. As for me, I sailed through the lobby unchecked, searching for Elgin. After eighteen years, he could hardly be expected to look the same, and yet of course that's just what I did expect: a tall, whip-thin, irritable young man with an impossibly large head, a beaked nose, and a dense, unbalanced mass of black curly hair looming like a ziggurat over his brow. He used to wave it back off his forehead with the flat of his hand. I remembered that now, as I made my way toward the gate—that little flip of his hand, ironical in its way, as if the hand was fully conscious of itself as it went about its business, and slightly wearied by itself too. That was the impression. He'd enter the classroom like a mourner, ten minutes late, hunched at the shoulders, his voice a knot of phlegm at the back of his throat. His jeans were tight and black. Perhaps they had started out blue, but on Elgin they were black. His eyes were black too, profoundly so; they drooped at half-mast in their sockets. His second wife, Janet, had left him over the holidays that year. Elgin was forty at the time, more or less the same age I am now, and about twelve years older than Janet herself—who had been his student, of course. So had Louise. Everyone had been Elgin's student. It was a process, apparently, that never ended.

But it had ended for Janet. The loss of her was right there on his face, Tuesdays and Thursdays, two to four. The rest of the week was formless, meandering. Perhaps for Elgin too. Perhaps he too had to gird himself for class, as Laura and I did, with coffee and sugar, bracing for the exertion, the hail of commandments he'd hurl down from his high, solitary mount. Here were the lessons he'd learned writing his slender, nasty, penetrating books: He dared us to absorb them. Well, we tried. Meekly we'd turn in our stories, once a week, piling our hopes on a corner of his desk. Elgin threw them in his briefcase and snapped it shut. Then he carried our futures home with him, back to his unimaginable study in his unimaginable house in the unimaginable hills, where he scrawled out our fates in the margins with his black pen.

Ask Laura what that time was like. How after three weeks we were all trying to write like Elgin wrote, talk like Elgin talked. Ask Laura about the anxiety of influence. My life, in Laura's view, has too much of both. But then whose doesn't?

And now here he was, emerging from the accordion ramp with his coat folded over his arm, like any befuddled tourist. "Elgin?"

"What time is it here?" Elgin said at once, looking not at me but at his watch.

"Four-fifteen."

"That late?" He continued to peer down at his watch, rather hopelessly, as if whatever time was written there was in a foreign language. My immediate impression was that he looked more or less the same as I remembered, though the more I examined him—his pouchy white face, his bony, spotted hands, a new precipitous tilt to his shoulders—the less in fact this seemed true. "Fucking hell."

"How was your flight?"

He gave me an ironic grimace, whether in response to the substance of my question or to its conventionality, I didn't know.

"It *is* hard to get here," I offered helpfully. "No direct connections, so you wind up bouncing around half a dozen regional hubs. And then there's the weather. Arctic fronts. Canadian winds. The occasional nor'easter. It's relentless. Laura says if it weren't for—"

"How long's the drive?" Elgin asked.

"Up to the college? About two hours."

"I'll be right back."

I am not a great detail man, but I was responsible for Elgin's visit, so while he was in the bathroom, I busied myself attending to my administrative duties where Elgin was concerned: I confirmed his seat on the return flight the next afternoon; I checked the weather forecast on the CNN monitor; I called Laura on the cell phone to tell her we were on our way. At the same time I casually inspected Elgin's bag, trying to read it—for I was an inveterate close reader, Elgin had seen to that—to decode, from the bumps and decavities in the nylon, what the next twenty-four hours might be like. Laura, meanwhile, didn't seem to be home. This struck me as odd. She had worked out an ambitious dinner with a festive, hot-climate theme, one that required care and timing. Perhaps she had forgotten an ingredient and had to run out to the market. Meanwhile the weather map wasn't looking so great either.

Then Elgin returned, his face damp and his eyes slightly more alert, and I stuck the phone in my pocket and grabbed his bag and we made our way through the swooshing doors and out toward the parking lot. "So," Elgin said, buttoning his coat, "here we are in Hamilton."

"Here we are in Hamilton," I agreed.

"Like it much?"

"No, not really."

"Well," he said, "why would you?"

Immediately I was sorry I had not invited Elgin to visit years before. If only I had made different choices, I thought. Or else the same choices, but more quickly, more concisely. I might have crammed a lot more life into my life.

"Of course it's very beautiful," he said, "give it credit. Like over there." He nodded toward the white, jagged slopes beyond the runways. "What do they call those?"

"Mountains, I think."

It was just a little reflexive joke, the sort I made all the time, irritating Laura and for all I know everyone else, but Elgin snorted appreciatively through his nose. I had gotten his attention. It's difficult to describe how happy that made me.

"Actually," I said, "they're the Whites." Though of course they weren't. They were the Greens. The Whites, I realized at once, lay to the east. And the Adirondacks, they were around here somewhere too. But where? In an effort to cut down on any more tedious and unnecessary misinformation, I confessed, "The truth is I'm not much of a mountain person. My wife's the one to ask."

"Ah," Elgin said mildly.

"People tell me to try harder to get into it. Nature I mean. The thing to do, they say, is take up skiing or snowshoes or kayaks or whatever. Basically the idea is to exhaust yourself and go to bed early, so you won't notice how little there is to do."

"Remind me your wife's name," Elgin said.

"Laura. Laura Eisenman. She was in my class."

"Laura Eisenman."

"Here's the car." I opened the trunk and tried, by force of mental exertion, to will away the mess that confronted us—the broken toys, the frozen leaves, the tennis balls with their pale, fuzzy nimbuses, the crumpled juice boxes with their mutilated straws. "I apologize for all the dog hair. A dog is pretty much standard equipment around here."

"I don't mind," Elgin said.

"You prefer cats, though. It's clear from the stories. The thing is, I do too. The dog was Laura's idea. For the kids. I hate dogs." This wasn't entirely true, but, if you'll bear with me here, it wasn't exactly a lie either. Because in that moment, watching Elgin fold himself into the front seat, I *did* hate dogs—not my dog per se (his name, as it happened, was also Elgin), whom after some initial resistance I had come to adore, but dogs as genus and species, dogs as *signifying objects,* as my colleagues like to say.

"You'd go crazy," I said, with a sudden vehemence that surprised even me. "Living here. It would bore you to tears."

He shrugged. The issue did not appear to engage him one way or the other. Why should it? I was the one who lived here, not Elgin. Tomorrow, as I'd just confirmed at the flight counter, Elgin would arrive back in San Francisco, where the coffee was good and the population diverse and flowers grew all through the winter, and where on sunny days, and they were all sunny days in my mind, the sailboats glittered like pearls against the wide blue throat of the bay. Life out there was a great, tangled garden full of languorous cats and trellised vines. Meanwhile here the ground was only just beginning to thaw. In another few weeks it would be mud season, and a month or so after that would come a fleeting and anemic spring. I was thirty-eight years old. I was still just beginning, poking my way through the chrysalis, in transition to whatever my life, my actual and singular life, would be. This is what I tried to explain to Laura, when I came home from the vasectomy. These next few years were critical for me. Anything could happen. *This guy might be the real thing . . .*

"That piece about the doctor," Elgin said suddenly. "The doctor who learns to paint. That was hers?"

I knew at once the story he meant. Perhaps I should have been surprised that he remembered it, but I wasn't. After all, we remembered every word from that class; why shouldn't he?

"Right," I said. "That was Laura's."

"Strong piece."

"Thank you," I said, rolling down the window to pay the parking attendant, though of course I realized, even at the time, that the compliment wasn't intended for me. "She loved your class, you know. We all did. I can't tell you how much."

Elgin, as if on cue, waved his hair back with his hand. Both hair and hand were white now, and somewhat less substantial than I remembered; both appeared to tremble in the sudden wind. The parking attendant was a teenager with an impressive constellation of pimples and an Adam's apple the size of a pomegranate. To watch him making change in his glass booth was somehow cause for sadness. A wave of tender feeling rolled through me, not just for him but for all of us in our glass boxes, the young, the old, and those, like me and Laura, suspended between, and as I rebuckled my seatbelt, waiting for the gate's long arm to rise, everything I wanted to say to Elgin, even the things I had vowed not to say, had vowed never to say, rose with it. "I'd love to talk to you about my book," I heard myself tell him.

"Sure thing," Elgin said.

"I mean later, of course. If there's time. It's just . . . you have no idea how much trouble it caused me. I almost gave up on it half a dozen times. I kept losing the thread. I'm not sure it even has one. I mean, talk about loving the difficult," I added, with a rueful frown, as if the phrase had only just come to me.

"Mmm?"

I was disappointed, of course, that Elgin didn't appear to recognize the line, and I had to work for a moment to suppress that, but otherwise I was beginning to feel pretty good about how it was all going. Which is to say, it was going approximately how I'd pictured it going—the two of us, mentor and protégé, soaring through the frozen midday light, talking about the vagaries and vicissitudes of fortune. Soon we would arrive at the campus auditorium, which I knew for a fact would be jammed. I had required my classes to attend, and had inveigled my colleagues in the literature division to do the same. Exactly two hours and nineteen minutes from now, I would stride to the lectern, give one of those calm, authoritative, professorial nods to signal an end to all the surface buzz, and then read the introduction I had been working on in both the back and front quadrants of my mind for, oh, half of my life now, laying out the parameters of Elgin's accomplishments, tracing the tendrils of his influence, and my colleagues would sit there nodding pleasantly in their impassive, obligatory way, the chair, the senior faculty, the tenure committee, happier than they'd expected to be playing hooky from their warm, isolated houses, even if it meant having to listen to some arty little stories by this fellow they'd never heard of. And then Elgin would begin to read, in that peculiar adenoidal singsong that was his style, and that had invisibly and unconsciously morphed over the years to become—I realized it only now—my own, and after the initial strangeness had passed, the room would grow very quiet and tense, as if some large meteorological event were underway . . . the air thinning out, the pressure of our attention rising into the red . . . and there would be cold gusts, and jagged flashes of light, and oscillating interludes of thunder and stillness . . . and abruptly, before proper shelter could be found, the story would darken around us, and, with a shudder and crack, rain down on our heads. That was the effect, when he was at his best. As if the world around you was giving way. Going wrong. And then all would be silent, so silent that we would hear the soft thud of the cover closing, and the rippling sigh the pages made, before we'd realize that the reading was over, and rouse ourselves at last to add the slow gratuitous thunder of applause. Afterwards, I'd stand there patiently while Elgin received his tributes, and signed old copies of his books with their yellowed jackets, and endured the usual chitchat with the pink-faced emeritus types in the front row, who liked to weigh in on these things, and then, before the twilight tedium could become too entrenched, I'd rescue Elgin with a silent tap on the shoulder and another meaningful nod, and drive him back to our picturesque little farmhouse on the south end of town, and there would be Laura in the black Yves St. Laurent dress she never gets to wear, and the amber necklace I'd bought her in Prague which ditto, and there would be the olives and the goat cheese and the Shiraz, and the dog and the children to be fussed over, and three plates laid out in the aspiring candlelight, and at some point in the meal, between, say, the rich marrowy osso bucco and the dewy wedge of homemade flan, I would tell Elgin how important he had been to all of us, not just his work but the whole high and rigorous aesthetic it embodied; and Laura, presuming her day at the clinic had gone well and the meal to which she'd sacrificed a lot more time than she'd have liked had been properly appreciated, would, one could only hope, chime in too along not-too-dissimilar lines, and as Elgin began to fidget in embarrassment I would proceed to tell him the truth I had brought him three thousand miles to hear: that nothing in my life had approached the joy of reading those seven words he had written in response to my book.

Of course it wasn't the *whole* truth. The *whole* truth, which I would not confide to Elgin, was that my editor had no intention of printing his blurb on the jacket. The feeling at the house, according to my editor, was that in the current climate the name Elgin Ricks would sell approximately zero books. That was the feeling at the house. The feeling at *my* house was that in a better world, my editor and all his corporate colleagues would be downsized into oblivion, and a new race of two-legged, enlightened, writer-friendly beings would walk the earth. But let's face it, when it came to oblivion, their house was a good deal safer than our house, as Laura would be the first to remind me.

Speaking of climate: it was getting rather nasty by the time we hit Route 4. The clouds overhead looked bloated and gray, like corpses floating in a pool. We drove for a while without speaking. I had turned down the heater but apparently not all the way: a light confetti of decaying leaves came trickling merrily through the vents. Fortunately Elgin didn't see it. He was gazing out the window, breathing noisily through his mouth. A pale oval of fog was spreading across the glass. The tape had arrived at the end of Act One, Scene IV. The King was saying "I have begun to plant thee, and will labor to make thee full of growing," and then Banquo, or was it Macbeth, replied "There if I grow, the harvest is your own," and then whatever came next I didn't quite manage to hear, because Elgin, his great head lolling like a buoy, gave out with the first in a series of violent, peremptory snores.

II

The Visiting Writer was beat. It had been a long flight. More accurately, an extended series of short flights. The last was one of those twelve-seat puddle jumpers where there's no toilet or food and you sit there clutching your coat on your lap like a penitent. Fortunately the Visiting Writer had taken a couple of Percocets for his ankle on the previous flight, along with three tiny blue bottles of Bombay gin. These had helped dull the arthritic throb in his ankle. Also the pain in his head from reading J.'s galleys. Not that his novel was so terrible, as novels go. It was just bad in the usual way: forced in its events, padded in its style, narrow in its focus, shot through with evasions and deferrals. What did it matter? Who read novels at this point anyway? A vulgar, decadent, pox-ridden form. Still, they kept going off to their little colleges and colonies, scribbling away. You couldn't stop them.

Coming down the ramp he felt all scrambled up, out of scale. The airport was a plastic model of an airport. The mountains were a wide-angle photograph of mountains. Christ, but flying makes you submissive, the Visiting Writer thought. He'd begun to dread these rough passages from one place to another. Pia claimed he was growing more delicate by the day, while for her—she'd hardly needed to add, but did anyway—it was the opposite. But then Pia was twenty-seven: hard-bodied, unsentimental. That was what he liked about her. On the other hand, he was beginning to feel in *need* of some softness, some sentiment. Maybe it was time to end things there, he thought, veering toward the john, and get back to the business of being a lonely old guy who lived alone, something he was good at.

He felt better at the urinal as he undid his pants. There were men on both sides of him, grown men, with hairs in their ears, air-ing it out, letting fly. There was nothing delicate about it. They made a hell of a noise. Then came the automatic flusher like a round of applause, and the warm, roaring benediction of the hand dryer. Yes, it was an affirmation, the men's room, a return to the species's first principles. He'd have liked to stay there a lot longer. But he shouldered his bag and headed for the exit instead, which was where he saw J.

Right away he knew it was true: J. must have been his student once. He could see it in the younger man's face, that avid, greedy, acolyte sheen, that proprietary glimmer. It made him tired. Meanwhile J. stood there pumping his hand and looking him over hungrily. He felt like an old whore.

"Elgin." J.'s tone was serious, ceremonial. "It's so . . . so . . ."

"Hey," he said. "How you doing?"

A young woman forced her way around them, pushing a stroller. The Visiting Writer remembered that he had promised to call his oldest daughter at noon, before she left for her psychopharmacologist's office in Palo Alto. He sensed it was already too late. Around them in the toy airport stood various toy people in bulky coats and ugly sweaters. All had mastered that heartland trick of looking at once pale, red-faced, dwarfish, and obese. "What time is it here?" he asked.

"Time? Four-fifteen."

He did the calculations. "Fucking hell."

J. went ahead and started asking about his flight, the way one does, so the Visiting Writer excused himself and went back to the men's room, the way one also does, especially if one has a low threshold for gin-and-Percocet. There he stood at the sink with his eyes closed, waiting for the numbing insanity of travel to pass. In a moment, he knew, he'd have to get back to the business of chatting up J., his host, for whose mediocrity the Visiting Writer was apparently to be held responsible. It wasn't fair, but it was the case. So too with his other ex-students, and, though the categories overlapped, his ex-wives. Also his daughters, and their intractable depressions. This was his penalty, he thought, for consorting too long with the young. This was the toll they exacted. You had to go on giving to them, attending to their bottomless needs, until you had nothing left. Turn your back and they came stalking after you like Frankenstein's creature, long-faced and patricidal, seeking redress. Not that he blamed them. The Visiting Writer himself had had a mentor once, Harvey Dahlberg, the poet, back at Cornell, whom he'd loved, worshipped, until his first book came out, and that fat little fuck Harvey couldn't even rouse himself from the stupor of his petty, lethargic, small-time existence to acknowledge the thing until two years later. And then what had his note said? *A lot of people will call this the real thing.* But not Harvey, of course. Harvey called it *a worthy first effort.* Well, that was the way you mentored in those days: you ate your young. Nowadays it was even worse. Now you were required to love them, to pamper them. Now, like Jesus Christ, you had to dangle before them with your ribs showing, and let them eat *you.* Even those, like J., whom you hardly remembered.

Still, there were selfish reasons to be nice to J. too. There was the reading fee, higher than anything he'd received in years. There was that girl he'd married, who had been his student too. Laura. That one he remembered. Finally, there was J.'s editor down in New York, who had sent along a nice handwritten note with the galleys, inviting him for drinks next time he was in town. Okay, it wasn't lunch, but he wasn't a hot young thing anymore, he didn't write memoirs, or cinematic novels about lawyers; he wrote stories, short ones, taut and lean, and not many even of those. Why bother? The glossy magazines had gone taut and lean themselves. As for his publishers, the last contract, for a novel he'd never written, had been quietly and consensually euthanized three years back. The phrase "work in progress"—as in, "we prefer you to read not from old work but from work in progress"—had begun to strike the Visiting Writer as increasingly fanciful, even cruel. There was work, a great deal of work, but was there progress? He pushed his way out of the men's room and into the garish, overlit terminal, where people were lined up at the counters looking for a way out, and J., his long pale face like a mirror, waited by the sliding doors, fingering his keys.

III

I grew up in California, so naturally I was curious about snow at first, and marveled at the beauty of it, and the great swooning silence that attended its falling, but then my curiosity was satisfied and I was ready to move on. Unfortunately the snow up here is never in a hurry to move on. The snow, having lugged itself across Canada and over the Great Lakes, tends to slow down after it arrives, to settle in and put up its feet and declare a holiday. That's what it was doing on our way home from the airport. Unpacking its bags, making itself comfortable. I watched it sweep in from the northwest, skid across the icy lake, bump into the foothills behind us, and come circling back. I had lived in this valley long enough to form two paradoxical conclusions: a) the snow wasn't going to stop anytime soon, and b) Elgin's reading would go on anyway, as planned. Because up here you didn't let the bad weather stop you. The plows went to work, and so did you: you put on your boots, zipped up your parka, shoveled a path to the car, loaded your three or four kids onto the schoolbus, and got on with it. That was the New England spirit, can-do and pragmatic, unbowed. Live free or die. There was a lot of New England spirit up here in New England. It was rather hateful in some ways but it was also semi-admirable, a point I readily conceded to Elgin as we fishtailed through the parking lot, struggled out of the car, and began to slog our way toward the auditorium. Only Elgin did not seem to hear me. He was bent double against the wind, squinting to make out the hand-lettered sign taped to the door, the one that said READING CANCELED DUE TO WEATHER.

"I don't believe this," I announced, twenty minutes later, in the downstairs lounge of the Turtle & Shamrock. "This can't be happening."

Elgin signaled to the waitress for a refill on his gin. "On the contrary," he said.

"My kids'll be happy, anyway."

"Christ, look out there. It's like a Russian novel."

"They love the snow, my kids. They think it's cool."

Elgin nodded, gazing out the window. He did not appear to be having such a bad time, though I could well have been wrong about that.

"To me," I said, "it would be cooler to have the reading. Not having readings is what we're used to up here. That's not cool. The cool thing would be to have it."

Elgin lifted his glass. "What's that line in Hardy? *The worthy encompassed by the inevitable*?"

"I've never read Hardy."

"Ah."

"Do you think I should? I hear his late work particularly is really amazing."

"Who knows," Elgin said irritably. "I stopped telling people who they should read a long time ago."

"Don't you find it hard to read great stuff when you're writing? There's this temptation to steal things."

"I should never have left the northeast," Elgin declared abruptly, shutting down our little Writers at Work interview before it could get started. "I should have moved up here, found an old house with a wood stove, and written some books. Wear a plaid shirt. Split some logs. I've never split a log in my life."

"Me neither," I said. "This guy down the road brings it over. All I do is write a check."

In the face of this disclosure Elgin shrugged, and gave his gin his full attention. I could feel the visit beginning to wobble. There was too much of something, or not enough of something else. What was needed was structure, something solid and workaday to which we could both react. But what? Laura would know, I thought. I drew out my cell phone and hit the programmed number for home. The tiny screen grew frantic with light. "Where is she? She was supposed to be home dealing with dinner."

Elgin had turned from the window to survey the room, inspecting the ambience of the place, such as it was, the wood beams and dartboards and stuffed animal heads on the walls.

"Hi, it's me, where are you? They canceled the reading so we walked over to the pub to wait out the storm. I'm getting worried about you so call when you get this, okay?"

"Is that a moose?" Elgin was staring at the great antlered head over the booth next to ours.

"Yeah, I think so. That's a moose alright."

"Get a lot of them up here?"

"Sure. They're all over the mountain. Of course they're killers, you know."

"How's that?"

"Well, they're incredibly big and dumb and slow, and they like nothing better than to wander out into the road and let you hit them. Then, because they're so tall, you wind up cutting their legs out from under them, so they come crashing through your windshield and crush you flat. It's a passive-aggressive form of murder."

"No kidding." Elgin stared up at the moose head again, as if contemplating the risk of sitting below it.

"Speaking of which," I said, "can I say one more time how sorry I am about this? You have no idea how much work I put into this event. How many boring emails went back and forth with various administrators, lining it all up."

"I don't do email," he said.

"I don't blame you. It eats up half my time at the computer these days."

"I don't do computers either."

I could tell from these automatic-sounding declarations that this was not exactly a fresh or stimulating subject area for Elgin.

"Insidious instrument," he said. "Sheer indulgence."

"I suppose you're right."

"You write a bad line, and the machine says, there there, it's okay, just save it, you'll fix it later. Everything that's bad can be made good. No wonder they're so popular. An honest machine would tell you the truth. Most bad lines can't be fixed. Or shouldn't be. You've got to hack them away. Any shmuck with hurt feelings can write. The art's in the hacking away."

"I suppose you're right," I said again.

Even as the phrase left my mouth, I wanted to call it back. "Suppose" was a soft word. A bad word. When had I stopped living my life and begun supposing it?

Elgin had fallen silent. He glared at the moose head pensively, as if deciding whether that too was something to be hacked away. The waitress brought us another round; I don't know why. I'd had two already, and was not prepared to go on. The silence grew and stretched. Scrolling through my mental file of all the things I'd decided to ask Elgin when I finally had him to myself,

I found that now, with the man before me, I could not identify a single question. The hard drive was empty. Or was it too full? My brain's cursor had frozen up tight. All at once, with the snow and the gin and the reading called off and Laura not home, I felt the day and all its precious freight begin to skid away from me, to go silently and relentlessly wrong.

"Listen," I said, "I'm thinking I should probably call the dean while I'm still sober. We can reschedule. It's not that difficult, presuming we can find a suitable room."

"Hopeless," Elgin informed the moose.

"No, no, it'll be fine. Tomorrow's Friday, of course, which isn't ideal, a lot of people go away on the weekends. But we'll get a crowd."

"I'm going home tomorrow," Elgin said. He patted the ticket in his pocket. "Two o'clock. Nonrefundable."

"We'll do it in the morning then."

"You must be joking. I don't read in the morning. I don't even see in the morning."

"Elgin," I said, struggling to flatten the quaver in my voice, "we're paying you fifteen hundred dollars. Plus expenses."

"Don't feel bad. You did the best you could. Of course in the old days," he mused, "I never went anywhere for less than two grand."

In the old days, I wanted to say, you were still publishing books.

"Anyway it's just a college reading," he said. "Who cares? None of these kids have even heard of me."

"Sure they have," I said.

I'd spoken quickly, but perhaps not quickly enough. Elgin made that appreciative snort again through his nose, only this time it didn't sound entirely appreciative. I was beginning to wonder if it had been entirely appreciative the first time either.

"It's true. I've told them all about you."

"Told them what?" he said. "That I was the best writer in America they were never going to hear of?"

"He said you were the best writer in America, period."

Both of us turned around. "Hey, Valerie," I said.

"Hi, Professor Jackson."

"I didn't know you were old enough to drink here."

"I'm not," she said. "When the reading got canceled I just wandered over to visit my friend."

Valerie Ruane, it should be said, was not my most original student, but she was among the brightest and most interesting. She had a clear unforced style, and an unusually grave, thoughtful way of voicing unusually grave, thoughtful opinions in class, opinions I had come to trust at least as well as I trusted my own. Of course her beauty was a problem we all had to contend with. Valerie herself did what she could, dressing in baggy clothes, wearing blockish thick-lensed glasses, tying back her luxuriant red hair in a tight, severe, unflattering bun; but there were aspects of her physicality that she was unable, or perhaps unwilling, to negate, and so as a general rule I had found it useful to never quite look at Valerie Ruane. Instead I simply inclined my head in her general direction, suggesting the appearance of someone listening intently while maintaining, on a deeper level, several layers of numbing insulation from the filigreed heat element of her actual self. This not-quite-looking was a technique I had perfected over the long years of my marriage, one I now practiced more or less indiscriminately—with Laura, for example, and with myself too.

Nevertheless, I was looking at Valerie now. In her black pea coat and checkerboard scarf Valerie stood framed against the window, smiling expectantly. For a moment, the Rorschach of her freckles and the blizzard whirling behind her seemed to merge into one washy-wavy screen of static, separating our little focus group from the boring public access channels all around us—the town, the college, the friend she had come to see. "Valerie," I said, "meet Elgin Ricks."

"I know who you are." She frowned. "He also said he learned more from you in a week than he learned from all his other teachers combined."

"Sad comment," Elgin said. "But no doubt true."

"Valerie here's my best student," I heard myself crow to Elgin. "You're going to be hearing a lot from her one of these days."

As if in evidence of this claim, I took Valerie's hand and presented it, that marbled trophy, to our collective gaze. Naturally I had memorized all the harassment guidelines and so was as shocked as anyone to discover this twenty-year-old hand, with its long fine bone structure and its pale, puffy nails, in such close contact with my own. How had that happened? And why was I clutching it so tightly? I let it go almost at once, wincing at the sound her knuckles made when they hit the table, and went back to my habitual mode of not-quite-looking at Valerie, and not-quite-touching her either.

"I really wanted to hear you read," Valerie told Elgin. "I've read, like, all your stories. They're amazing."

"Ah." Smiling darkly, he looked down at his drink.

"That one from your first book? When the cab driver bursts into tears at the end? I loved that."

"Me too," I could not refrain from adding. Because I did. I had loved it when I was Valerie's age, and I still loved it now.

"And then he just sits there in the rain with the wipers going. And the cars are all passing him on the right and left. It's exquisite. It reminded me of that scene in—"

"I know," Elgin said mournfully, ducking his large head. "Grand larceny. I should have been taken out and hung for that."

"No no," Valerie said. "It made me cry. People my age, we never write like that. We're not hungry enough. We've been too, I don't know, *gratified* or something. We're just not desperate enough."

"You will be," Elgin said. "Rest assured. You won't be able to help it."

Right then the cell phone rang. It was Laura. The reception was very poor, however, in the Turtle & Shamrock, and I could not hear everything she was saying, not with Valerie and Elgin's debate on literary ethics going on at the same table, Elgin still grimacing into his drink, and Valerie still talking, as if reassuring a child about a story he'd brought home from school, that no, it was a very good piece, very honest and powerful, with a harsh sort of beauty, and besides, Professor Jackson says that writers are always taking things from other writers, that that's just the way it works, you never know when you're being original and when you're just channeling your influences, so you shouldn't worry so much about . . .

"I think it's starting to let up," I said. "We should go."

"Go where?" Valerie asked brightly. "Is there some faculty dinner for Mr. Ricks?"

"The bill always comes," Elgin sighed.

"Actually, we were planning to have you over to the house. Just Laura and me. We figured we'd try to spare you the old rigmarole."

"Perfect," Elgin said, a bit louder than necessary. "Some new rigmarole."

"You'll have fun," Valerie assured him. "His wife's the best cook in town. Everyone says so."

"They do?" I asked.

"She cooked that Indian meal for your junior seminar last year, remember? They still talk about it."

"Maybe we should bring along the young lady," Elgin suggested, finishing off his gin. "She's full of hunger. She said so herself."

"I didn't mean that sort of—"

"Hunger is hunger, young lady. One either has it or one doesn't. And you do. Anyone can see how desperate you are for a good, like, meal."

Valerie Ruane turned scarlet.

"I'm fine," she said, so gamely and with such preternatural composure that I nearly embraced her, not just her hand but her whole exquisite and forbidden self. Looking back, I wish I had. I wish I had embraced that girl, and then wrung Elgin's long, arrogant neck, and then wandered out into the snow to die like that hero—or was he the villain?—in D.H. Lawrence.

"Yes, but you'll be finer if you come. Tell her," Elgin said to me. "Tell her she'll be finer if she comes. You're her teacher. Use your influence."

"You'll be finer if you come," I said.

The worthy encompassed by the inevitable.

"I'll be fine," Valerie reminded us all, "either way."

IV

The Visiting Writer was far enough under the influence himself that by the time they pulled up to the farmhouse, he was reasonably certain he was dreaming. The snow shushing beneath the tires, the warm, tactile proximity of this young girl beside him, forming her pale clouds of breath, the murmur of oddly familiar voices speaking words he knows he knows *(. . . who then shall blame his pestered senses . . . when all that is within him does condemn itself for being there?)* . . . yes it was a dream, only that; if by no other means he could tell by his hard-on. Lately his hard-ons were more accessible in dreams than in that other demanding arena, real life. Well, what could you do? The body had a mind of its own. At the moment, his was focused exclusively on that of the girl beside him: her fleecy hair, her even, pliant breaths, and so it was terrifically irritating when J. screeched to a halt, and his door flew open, inviting into the car an unwelcome amount of snow.

"I don't get it. She's supposed to be home."

"I bet she's waiting out the storm somewhere," the girl said. "That's what I'd do."

The Visiting Writer opened one eye, frowned, and snuggled imperceptibly closer to this sensible girl. Her coat was downy and soft. Her head smelled of shampoo. Her hands were folded neatly over her seatbelt, which was, he observed, carefully buckled. Not a wild generation. She'd said so herself. Thoughtful, polite. Good homes, good schools, even good drugs. Smart drugs. His daughters too. So far their transgressions were still small ones. They did not know about the other kind, not yet, the kind you couldn't medicate away.

"Well, let's go in and wait. Maybe there's a message. Elgin?"

"I think Mr. Ricks is asleep."

"Oh."

"Should we wake him up, do you think? He looks so comfortable."

The Visiting Writer debated for a while which would be more dignified: to go on pretending to be asleep or to go on pretending, as he had since he'd stepped off the plane, that he was awake. All things being equal, it was probably better to keep moving. Sleep was an indulgence. At his age, you had to keep the body limber, or else it began to stiffen around you like a cast. When in doubt, follow the girl.

"Are we there?" he asked froggily.

V

It's shameful to admit, but when I walked in and turned on the lights, I was not quite so worried about Laura and the kids as I probably should have been. I was much too busy blaming them for the condition of the place, both for the presence of so many unwanted things—the plastic toys that littered the coffee table, the ice skates, shorn of their rubber guards, tangled on the rug, the cereal bowls teetering precariously in the sink—as well as for the absence of so many desired ones. The fire that wasn't going in the fireplace, the pots that weren't bubbling musically on the stove, the wine that wasn't uncorked and breathing on the counter, the goat cheese that hadn't been set out to ripen on a ceramic plate . . . I blamed Laura and the kids for these too. Above all, I blamed them for either turning me into or allowing me to become such a trivial, domesticated person as to even notice these unexpected presences and absences, let alone be enraged by them to the point where I was able to forget, for a moment anyway, that for all I knew Laura and the kids had been killed that day in a tragic, snowy crash—a death I would probably have welcomed, I'm ashamed to say, had I not been so eager to blame them for all these other things they had and hadn't done first.

"Well hello, you," gushed Valerie, for of course the dog had discovered us by now, and was treating all of us to her usual noisy, over-explicit welcome. "I'm happy to see you too."

"Nice dog," Elgin said politely, keeping his distance.

"What's your name, big fella?" Valerie asked, stooping over to ruffle the hair on his neck. "What do they call you? I bet it's a really sweet name, a sweet thing like you."

"We call him, uh, Joe. Joe the dog."

"Joe," Valerie said. She was looking directly at the ID tag on his collar, the one that read "Elgin." "I like that."

"Thanks."

"I like this house a lot too," she said. "You've got nice things. Even nicer than I pictured."

"Thanks," I said again, and because this seemed an insufficient response to the wondrous, gratifying image of Valerie Ruane lying around her dorm room in her nightshirt, trying to picture my things, I added, "I'd give you both a tour if it weren't such a mess."

"If you could just point me to the john," Elgin said.

"Right there."

"Ah."

Valerie and I watched him go. All at once, the moment felt oddly fateful and tense; we might have been watching a child head off to summer camp for the first time. *Our child.* In a sense we had both undertaken, back at the pub, to care for Elgin, to nourish and protect him on his sojourn through space. Soon, of course, he would need to individuate himself, to rebel and leave us and head off under his own power; but for now he was our responsibility, and we accepted that. The bathroom lock clicked shut. The compressor in the refrigerator began to hum. With a certain inevitability we turned to each other, Valerie and I, and exchanged a long look. I don't know what it meant. As I said, I was not used to looking at Valerie directly, it wasn't something I was good at or prepared for, and it's possible as a consequence that I may have stopped breathing for a moment or two. Valerie, for her part, didn't move. Her mouth formed a small inquisitive line. She appeared to be waiting for me to do something, something very simple and particular that could not be put into words. It hardly seemed possible that the thing Valerie was waiting for me to do was the same thing *I* was waiting for me to do, all the time knowing I would never do it, no way, not in my house, in front of my dog, with Elgin in the bathroom and my kids' Cheerios all bloated and shapeless in the sink, with tenure so close, and Laura so mysteriously far.

"What do you think?" I asked.

"About what?"

I shrugged. "You know. About Elgin."

"Oh." Her mouth tightened. "I don't know. He's okay. I love his stories, I really do. But he's kind of a creep."

"He is?"

"I guess all that gin back there didn't help. But he's got that sad older guy look. Also I don't like the way he's so jealous of you."

"You must be kidding."

"It's obvious. That's why he talks to you that way. He's afraid. He thinks he's all done, and you're just hitting your prime. It must be really hard to have your students pass you. No wonder he's so angry. It's probably also why he tried to feel me up in the car."

"Really?" *Are you sure that wasn't me?*

"Guys his age, it's almost like they can't help it. You get to the point where you can pretty much see it coming."

"What about guys my age?"

"Guys your age," Valerie said coolly, "have wives. Wives and kids."

"And does this make us different?"

"No," she said. "It just makes you act different."

"Most of us, I'm afraid, don't act much at all."

"Mmm."

People tend to look back on their student years as a period of great confusion. But we who teach know better: in fact it's a time of great clarity, the clarity of confidence, of fresh sight, newly discovered powers. The confusion comes later, when you've got more to lose, when your instincts, those double agents, can no longer be trusted to protect you from loss—to *want* to protect you—or tell the difference, if there is one, between a smoking, pitiable ruin and a standing house.

There was a whoosh of water from the bathroom. I looked down to discover that there was now almost no empty space between the point where Valerie left off and where I myself began.

The dog had begun to whine, his nails ticking back and forth on the wood floor. I waited for the crunch of tires in the driveway, the flare of high beams against the windows. Elgin was still in the bathroom. Good lord, was this what it was like, getting old? The man spent half his life in the bathroom, piddling around alone.

Soon that would be me, I thought. Soon that would be me.

"Come on," I whispered. "Let's hide."

VI

Gabe's hockey game started late because of the snow, and went into overtime. So we didn't get out of there until six. Then we had to stop at the drugstore for Jenna's cough syrup. By the time we got to the market they were out of veal. So the whole dinner had to be rethought, right there in the middle of Grand Union, with Gabe complaining about his coach and Jenna coming down with a fever, and that awful Melissa Tolman chattering away about the band concert coming up, and I kept thinking, I could have hired a babysitter and gone to Elgin's reading. It couldn't have been any worse than this. Or maybe it could. I used to like Elgin's work but as the years went by it began to seem thin and monotonous and a little self-indulgent. A lot of male writers strike me that way. It's beginning to happen to J. too, in this last book. Arrested development. But I don't read fiction anymore, so I shouldn't judge. If I could do better, I'd be doing better. And I'm not. So I should just shut up.

Plus there was that little incident at the Sugar House Motel. It was flattering at first, but then I realized that Elgin had sort of forgotten who I was about halfway through. He was having a rough time getting over Janet, I guess. That incident pretty much got me over my curiosity about what Professor Ricks was really like when you got to know him better.

But I could never talk about it. No chance. So all these years I've had to pretend to keep J. company in his wondering. Maybe that's what makes a good marriage. You both pretend to wonder the same things. Or maybe that's a bad marriage. You tell me.

Anyway there he was, the great and powerful Elgin Ricks, asleep on the sofa when we got home. He looked pretty awful, lying there in his black coat. Some men puff up as they age and some go all stringy; Elgin from the look of him had done both. Still, he was the same guy. It was there in the way he occupied the sofa. A looseness, a sort of amplitude. The guy's self-absorption was so complete it almost passed for pleasure. There was something attractive about it, even now.

This is Elgin, I told the kids quietly, as we all hovered over him. The man I told you about. The one who used to be Mommy and Daddy's teacher, way back when.

He doesn't look like a teacher, the kids said.

He's not a teacher anymore. Now he's just a man who sits around writing books.

You mean like Daddy does?

Sort of.

I think he's dead, Gabe whispered. He's not moving. And he smells bad.

We considered this topic for a while. Then we turned our attention to other, more pressing questions, like what was for supper, and whose turn it was to set the table, and who had to feed the dog, and who would take the first bath, and who this other pair of boots belonged to, the ones dripping onto the mud room carpet next to Daddy's—Elgin was wearing his neat black Italian shoes, which were ridiculously ill-suited to this weather; they were in the process of leaving wet spots on the sofa cushions—and hey where was Daddy anyway? I answered as many of these as I could while I was throwing dinner together, but those last two defeated me. Elgin had begun to stir. I don't know why, but all of a sudden I hated the blouse I was wearing. It made me look fat. I had to change right away. Quickly, before Elgin woke up, and before J. came out from wherever he was, and before the kids could think of another question to ask me, I ran down to the laundry room to fetch my new black silk blouse from the clothesline.

VII

No one would believe it if I wrote it as a story. I mean, I won't even try. Not until I graduate, anyway. Then, who knows, maybe I'll write it. What happened that night down in the laundry room. Sometimes it takes a while, Professor Jackson says, to get a handle on your material. Art requires perspective. You can't always get there from the inside.

I'll miss his class, though. I learned a lot from him. Someday, if I do actually become a writer, a real one I mean, it would be interesting to see him again. I don't know. Just to see.

VIII

It had been, the Visiting Writer thought later, flying home, one of his more vivid and peculiar dreams. His oldest daughter was crying. He did not know why. Daddy, she cried, you need to come out here right away. And so he had roused himself from the couch. Strangers were yelling at each other in another room. Their problems did not concern him. Dogs were barking. Amid all the noise, he heard his daughter's voice clearly, and followed it out to the field in front of the house.

At the edge of the field, half-hidden by trees, stood an enormous moose. Lie down, the moose said. You're having a dream.

IX

All I'll say in my own defense is that we were only holding hands. I'm not saying it couldn't have led to something more. I'm not saying that. But when Laura came in and found us in the laundry room, that's what we were doing.

Strictly speaking, I was holding Valerie's hand, but she wasn't holding mine. There's a very good chance that she was pulling hers away from me, in fact, even before Laura came in and found us in the laundry room.

Well, it was a confusing day.

Somehow we all wound up outside. Laura went first, and then I went chasing after her, and Valerie, I'm not sure, she might have been chasing me or she might have been chasing Laura, trying to explain, or she might have just been taking off on her own to get the hell out of there—you'd have to ask her—and then of course there was the dog, who knew that this was all just a loud, baroque game of tag for his benefit, and then the kids chasing after him in their pajamas and slippers, shouting "Elgin wait! Elgin wait!" . . . none of which was quite what I had in mind, frankly, when I'd invited Elgin to read at the college. Laura, of course, was in good shape from yoga; moreover, she'd grown up in the snow and was comfortable in it, so the running didn't appear to bother her. Doubtless too she was working harder at getting away than I was at catching her. For me, between the alcohol and my bad back and the various pounds I'd put on over the years, it was pretty slow going. So she would probably have beaten me to the car and gone skidding off down the driveway even if I hadn't tripped over something large and stationary that had been left in the field and gone sprawling face-first into the snow.

The dog found me first. Then, a few seconds later, I heard the panting of my children.

"Hey," I said, rolling onto my back. I did not feel ready to get up yet. "How was the game?"

"We lost," Gabe said. "And I played *terrible.*"

"Too bad."

"Where'd Mommy go?"

"She had to go do something. She'll be back soon."

"Where'd that other lady go? Did she go with Mommy?"

From where I lay I tried to crane my neck to find Valerie, but Valerie too was gone. "Maybe so."

"Where'd they go?" Jenna said.

"The store. I'm pretty sure she went to the store."

"*Told* you," Gabe said to Jenna, whose fat cheeks and tiny nose, so much like her mother's, were flushed scarlet from our little jog around the house.

"There's nothing to worry about, guys. Everything's fine. We're just trying to pull this dinner together so we can finally eat."

"We ate before," Gabe said. "After the game. Mommy bought us hot dogs."

"Lucky for you, then."

"What about the dead man?" Jenna asked.

"I'm not dead, honey. I'm just resting here a sec."

"No," Gabe said. "She means the man over there."

X

So he'd lain down in the snow. The air was cold and thin, the sky a riot of stars. He could not remember ever being so comfortable, so at rest. He understood that the clearing around him was something he had achieved for himself, that the trees which had once been there had been toppled by his own hands. No wonder he felt so tired. It was a pleasure just to lie there, to watch as, at the end of a play, all the major characters of his life's noisy, clanging skirmishes—his wives, his children, his parents, even old Harvey Dahlberg—emerged from the surrounding woods and took a bow. Then they were gone, and the trees began to move closer.

The moose stood in the starlight, its gaze mournful, remote. Somewhere far away a woman cried.

Daddy's dead, the children were whispering. He's not a teacher anymore. He's dead.

XI

He looked so peaceful I almost hated to disturb him. But it occurred to me that the children might be right for a change, and Elgin could be dead in front of my house. I poked at him. He didn't move. "Hey Elgin," I said.

The dog, thinking I was calling him, trotted over at once. He too gave Elgin a little poke. We waited for him to move. Some time passed. The children hovered in a tense, anticipatory way, but I could see they were growing bored with the whole dead man thing. They began to throw snowballs at each other. The snow had stopped falling, but the wind still whistled in the trees. It seemed to be speaking to me, teaching me a weird, thrilling new language. I felt cold and clear, beyond all sentiment. It occurred to me that I had killed Elgin Ricks, and I wasn't sorry. The extent of my not-sorriness was so profound it could only mean one thing: I had wanted to kill him, wanted to kill him all these years. *Needed* to kill him. Just as I had wanted, *needed,* to lose my wife. I had done everything I had secretly wanted to do. That was my breakthrough. And now I was free.

"Hey," Gabe said. "He moved his hand."

"No he didn't," said Jenna.

"Yes he did. See? He did it again."

"Go back in the house and get ready for bed," I told them.

"No," they said at once.

"Your slippers are soaked through. Go. And take the dog with you."

"Where's Mommy," they asked again. I was able to envision a day when I would grow tired of that particular question.

"Mommy'll be back soon."

After they were gone, Elgin coughed quietly and opened his eyes.

"I thought I heard a moose," he said.

"I doubt it. Moose don't generally make a lot of noise."

"Ah."

"Laura will be back in a little while. Then we'll eat."

"No hurry," Elgin said. "I'm fine right here."

"Me too. It's pretty peaceful, actually."

"You're right."

"I need to ask you something," I said.

"Look, if it's about your novel, I'd rather talk another time."

"It's about Laura," I said.

"What about her?"

"What happened to her? When we met, back at college, she was the best writer in the whole place. You said so yourself. Then in senior year she stopped finishing stuff. After that she stopped *starting* stuff. And now, I don't know, it's like she resents me for doing what she should have been doing all along."

"Why, you stupid fuck," Elgin said. "She gave you a gift."

"I don't think that was her intention."

"How do you know? How would *she* even know? Listen, take my word—if any of my ex-wives had given me what she's given you, I'd still be married to them." He frowned. "Actually, that's not true."

"So I'm what happened to her, is what you're saying."

Elgin was getting to his feet, brushing off his trousers. I did too. I looked behind us, at the dark shapes in the snow where our bodies had been.

"And you're what happened to me," I said.

"Want some advice?" He smiled darkly. "Don't waste your time with this shit. Get on with what matters."

"The work, you mean."

He laughed. He pushed in the knob of his watch to illuminate the time.

"I need to make a phone call," he said.

Well, it's a small town, and there isn't much entertainment available, so I guess if nothing else I provided some of that. Laura packed up the kids and moved to her sister's. Then, a few weeks later, she came back. The whole thing after all was strictly PG-13. Still, between Laura's reaction, my reaction to her reaction, Valerie's reaction to Laura's and my reactions—to say nothing of Elgin passing out in the snow, where he might have died of pneumonia had the kids not found him—there was plenty of embarrassment to go around.

The irony is they gave me tenure anyway. It turns out that the college likes a certain manageable quotient of scandal; it gives the place the appearance of liveliness. I had thought . . . well, what had I thought? I had thought too much, and acted too little, and then when I did act it was at the wrong time, in the wrong place. For years I had been observing my life through the wrong pair of eyes. No wonder it looked so blinkered, so small. Even my disasters could be read, next to Elgin's, as pale ones. Acceptable ones. After all, I'm still here. I inspire neither fear nor idolatry. I do not abuse myself or others, do not run off to Mexico, or trash my house, or show up drunk at department meetings. I do not walk into class twenty minutes late, with black rings under my eyes, and give vent to Shakespearean furies. No. I come early, and sit there with my mineral water in the quiet of the classroom, waiting, as I have always waited, for the sound of my voice to emerge.

About the Author

Robert Cohen is the author of three novels, *The Organ Builder, The Here and Now,* and *Inspired Sleep.* His short fiction has appeared in *Harper's, GQ, Paris Review, Ploughshares,* and other publications. His awards include a Lila Wallace–Reader's Digest Writer's Award, a Whiting Writers' Award, a Pushcart Prize, and the Ribalow Prize. He teaches at Middlebury College in Vermont, where he lives with his wife and sons.